AW hw

X $19.95
-L-   Williams, Rose, 1912-
F   A bridge for Judith
WIL

A BRIDGE FOR JUDITH

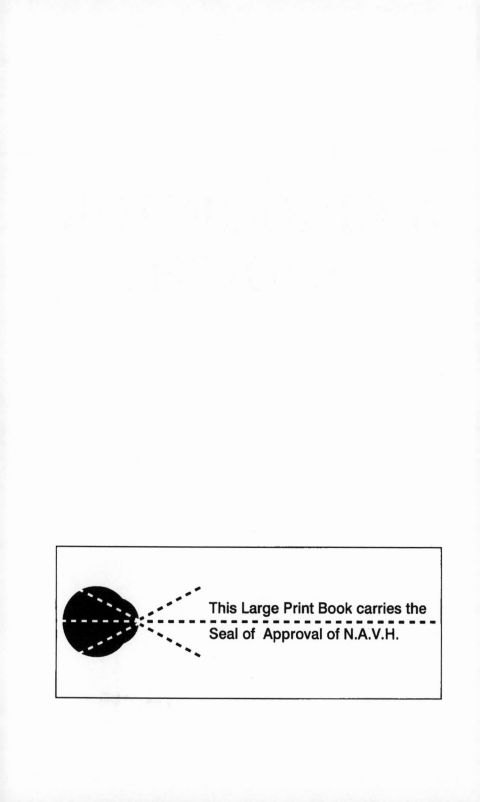

This Large Print Book carries the
Seal of Approval of N.A.V.H.

A BRIDGE FOR JUDITH

ROSE WILLIAMS

Thorndike Press • Thorndike, Maine

Copyright © 1968, by Arcadia House

Published in 1998 by arrangement with
Maureen Moran Agency.

Thorndike Large Print ® Candlelight Series.

The tree indicium is a trademark of Thorndike Press.

The text of this Large Print edition is unabridged.
Other aspects of the book may vary from the original edition.

Set in 16 pt. Plantin by Juanita Macdonald.

Printed in the United States on permanent paper.

Library of Congress Cataloging in Publication Data

Williams, Rose, 1912–
    A bridge for Judith / by Rose Williams.
        p.   cm.
    ISBN 0-7862-1644-1 (lg. print : hc : alk. paper)
    1. Large type books.   I. Title.
    [PR9199.3.R5996B75   1998]
    813´.54—dc21   98-30789

To Marilyn and Tom McGloan
— for obvious reasons!

CHAPTER ONE

All at once Judith Barnes realized she was alone on the wide steel girder that would provide part of the support for the superstructure of the bridge. Alan Fraser had been at her side only a moment before, but he had taken a few steps back to consult with Bud Stamers, the on-the-site engineer in charge of construction. With Alan beside her she'd felt no alarm, but now she was terrified.

The girder's surface was no more than two feet wide, and a moment of vertigo or a single wrong step could send her plunging down hundreds of feet into the rough gray water of the harbor below. Not until now had she been aware of the strong breeze on this day in late May. Even though the sun shone bleakly from behind the fleecy cumulus, it was by no means a pleasant afternoon. She heard Alan's crisp voice in conversation with the young engineer behind her, and she fought back the urge to scream out in terror for him to come to her.

Swallowing hard, she tried to obliterate her fears by concentrating on the view around her. The bridge was to join the city of Port Winter from west to east, and construction had begun at the west end on which they were now standing. At this point all the pillars to support the structure had been sunk in place across this narrow part of the harbor, and steel girders had been erected to connect the pillars halfway across the proposed span of the long bridge. Beyond that, tall cranes and swarms of steel-helmeted workers busily continued the construction. Alan Fraser, as chairman of the bridge authority, had come to make one of his regular inspections of the project. He'd invited Judith, as his secretary, to come along, since this day marked the halfway point in the building of the bridge. She had accepted his invitation with interest, not anticipating the peril she would face. The breeze tormented the skirt and coat of her tweed suit again, and she felt new panic.

Alan was still discussing some phase of construction in a worried tone, and she hesitated to intrude on him with what he would probably consider her silly fears. Not that the handsome, dark-haired young man was cruel or unthinking; actually, he was quite the reverse: too apt to show her consideration in most cases. It was just that he didn't know of her fear of heights and was so accustomed to striding out on the skeleton of the bridge he'd forgotten this was a new experience for her. Knowing all this, she pressed her elbows close to her sides and clasped her hands together tightly. Keeping the chin of her pert oval face up, she studied the opposite shore and the city beyond, realizing that should she be so foolhardy as to take a single glance down, she'd undoubtedly faint and topple into the grayish, foam-flecked water.

Ignoring a tugboat cutting through the water ahead, she concentrated on the opposite shore where a land construction team was already building the several ramps and roadways that would join with the bridge to shoot arteries of traffic to various sections of the city of a hundred thousand people. Port Winter was the chief New Hampshire port, indeed the only large one along the state's short coastline. It was an old city, dating back to the early New England settlers, and its ancient red brick buildings and quaint wooden houses stood out amid the newer structures of colorless gray office and apartment units.

These big buildings had little of the character of the area, and most of the people crowded into them were newcomers, testifying to the population explosion and the business boom the area had recently experienced under the dominant hand of financier S.C. North. The monument to this new growth and industry was the fifteen-story modern office building housing the head-quarters of the S.C. North enterprises and located at the foot of the ancient main street, King Street, named in honor of a long dead British monarch before the Republic came into being. A number of the city's streets were so named, forming links with the tight little island across the sea. Indeed, Port City's citizens visiting Britain always commented on this fact.

The passing tugboat blew its whistle to greet the workers on the bridge, and the sharp sound from so far below, plus the sight of the tugboat drifting off toward the open harbor, made her sway slightly again. Knowing it was a moment of crisis, she swiftly raised her eyes to the far horizon, the towering grain storage buildings that rivaled North's new skyscraper in height and the distant broad outlines of the city's two hospitals set high on hills, along with the spires of the Cathedral and Trinity Church, both a century or so old. Port Winter was a blend of the old with the new, and the bridge was meant to bring its citizens closer together by joining the sections built long ago on opposite sides of the wide harbor.

"Judith, I forgot about you! Are you all right?" It was Alan Fraser at her elbow, speaking in a solicitous tone.

With a great feeling of relief, she smiled at him over her shoulder. "I'll be honest! I was too frightened to move even an inch!"

He gasped her arm to steady her. "You poor kid! I was so busy checking with Bud about the delayed steel shipment I didn't give you a thought."

"It didn't matter!" she protested, not enjoying his embarrassment.

"You're not used to it out here," Alan went on. "I don't blame you for being scared. It's a long way up." Firmly but gently he guided her around so she was facing the shore. "Feel up to starting back?"

She attempted a smile and nodded. "Of course."

"We'll just take it slowly," he said as he led her back along the narrow girder.

"I don't mind as long as I have someone with me," she said, although her legs felt trembly and hollow.

Alan gave her a comforting smile. "I won't ask you out here again until I drive you across in my car."

She gave a small laugh. "That will be at least two years, if you keep up with your timetable."

"When you consider we've been working on this project for eighteen months now, it's not as long as it sounds," the young man at her side reminded her.

"That's true," she agreed. Her voice gained assurance as solid ground appeared under them. Now they were walking along the furrowed earth of the new construction area. Everywhere around them were noise and confusion and hurrying men and groaning equipment. The asphalt of the roadway approach to the bridge had not been laid yet.

Alan walked slowly beside her as they left the construction site and made their way to the huge parking area that served the bridge crew. His dark sedan was in the outmost row of parked cars.

"I'm going to take you back to the office," he said. "Then I'm going uptown to talk to Harvey Wheaton about this steel shipment. It's too long overdue. If we don't get part of it in a few days, we'll have a work stoppage."

She glanced at this worried face. "You can do without that."

"After the delays of last winter, we can't afford to lose a single day," he agreed. He was about a head taller than she and had dark, slightly curly hair. He rarely wore a hat, so his thin face was weathered by the sun and wind. He had the fine features of a scholar and had taken honors at college, but he also, surprisingly, had been something of an athlete as well. In fact, he'd been a star of the college track team. Since joining his father as a junior in the esteemed law firm of Fraser, Winslow and Stratton, he'd neglected sports. But he was a member of the Dover River Yacht Club and did have a slim, speedy sailboat. He'd taken Judith out on the lovely river more than once.

She said, "Still, it is wonderful to see the work half done."

He smiled. "When it looked as if we wouldn't get started at all for a while."

"I know," she agreed as she remembered those early days of controversy.

They had reached the car now. Alan opened the door for her, and she got in. He slid behind the wheel of the modest sedan and started the motor. In a few minutes they were heading up Prince Street toward the old bridge that was no longer able adequately to handle the traffic and the main section of the city.

As they drove he said, "Bud Stamers told me that Senator Lafferty has been out to view the construction quite a few times lately. What do you make of that?"

"Nothing good," she said with a resigned

expression on her attractive face. She was twenty-three and from the same background as Alan Fraser, and it was only a twist of fate that had cast her in the role of his secretary.

"I agree," he said, his eyes on the street ahead as they drove along a residential avenue which included two large public buildings, the Vocational School and the Historical Museum.

Judith's alert brown eyes were wide and questioning. "What can he be up to now?" she wanted to know.

Alan smiled grimly at the wheel. "He's not out to help us. Be certain of that. Don't forget he's been on S.C. North's payroll ever since he finished his term as Senator."

"I haven't forgotten," she agreed. She knew that any employee of the powerful S.C. North was apt to be opposed to the project her young boss was heading. There was a strong rumor that S.C. North had been annoyed at not being awarded the steel contract for the bridge and also that the stubborn financier had been displeased with the location of the bridge. Several people claimed he would have preferred a more direct route across the harbor which would have favored some of his business properties.

"Bud said he had a couple of city councilmen and some real estate people with him," Alan informed her.

"Sounds very solemn, official and typically underhanded!"

"You do not underestimate Senator Lafferty," Alan said with amusement. "I don't know whether it's that public life attracts the worst kind of pompous frauds or turns them into the type."

"I see it as a fifty-fifty thing," she said. "In the Senator's case it would be impossible for any career to spoil him. He must have always had the natural instincts of a crook from birth."

Alan nodded. "If you'll study that bloated red face of his, you'll notice the baby features behind it. I can see him now reaching craftily into the carriage next to him and stealing another baby's milk bottle."

"And he's never stopped since," Judith said, enjoying it. "Better watch out if the Senator has his eye on you."

He brought the car to a halt before the entrance to the old gray building opposite the modern fifteen-story edifice that housed the S.C. North companies. It was in this ancient structure, the lower floor of which was occupied by a staid bank and trust company, that Fraser, Winslow and Stratton had their offices. The only concession to modernism was a self-service elevator. And since this had not turned out a successful installation, it was generally regarded as a slow-moving error.

"Will you be back before the office closes?" Judith wanted to know as she prepared to get out of the car.

Alan had kept the motor running and was double-parked. "I'll try and get back by five to take any calls and sign those letters."

"Fine," she said with a bright smile of encouragement as she let herself out. "Good luck with Wheaton!"

Alan reached across to close the car door after her. "I have an idea I might need it," he said.

She hesitated a bare moment on the busy sidewalk and watched him drive off up the hill. Judith had known Alan since his school days; they had grown up together in houses built close together in the old city's exclusive Mount Pleasant district. They had spent a lot of time in each other's company before things had changed for her. So it was natural there should be a closeness between them not normally found in employer and secretary. With a sigh she turned and went into the shadowy hallway of the old building to take the elevator to the third floor offices of the law firm.

She remembered entering the building with her father before his death. There had been a stooped, elderly man operating the single elevator then. She and her father had been going to the offices of the insurance company on the second floor; the company that provided financial backing for her father's building projects. Wilfred Barnes had made a name for himself as a pioneer in putting up modern housing developments in the area. To Judith he seemed to be continually successful, so it had come as a rude shock that afternoon to learn that he was in a strapped financial position.

Oliver Wilson, the solemn, bespectacled head of the insurance firm, had regarded her father gravely across his desk while Judith sat by, not knowing what she was about to hear.

"You're on the verge of bankruptcy, Barnes," Oliver Wilson had bluntly told her father.

With his usual charm, her quiet father had parried the remark with a sad smile. "I've been through difficult times before and made out all right."

"I don't know whether that will be true this time," the insurance head had warned him. "We can't bail you out. We've extended your credit as far as we dare."

"I'll manage," her father had said with blithe assurance. And then, smiling across at her, "I wanted you to meet my daughter. She's taking a course in business administration at the university. I wondered if you could use her in the office during the summer holiday period?"

Oliver Wilson had brightened and studied her behind his glasses. "How is your typing and shorthand?"

"I've had plenty of experience in both," she'd assured him.

"We'll be glad to have you, then," he'd agreed.

So it had been settled, and she'd worked all that summer in this same building.

Somehow her father had kept the business going through that summer and into the beginning of the next year. Judith had wondered what was happening but hadn't had much chance to discuss it with him. In fact, he discouraged her on the few occasions when they were alone together. And when her mother was present, she didn't dare risk involving her in the worry. Millicent Barnes had been the only child of elderly parents and, along with a fragile, wistful beauty that had faded early, she'd inherited a delicate constitution and bad nerves.

So she was ill-prepared for the heart attack that suddenly took Wilfred Barnes off. Judith, although heartbroken, was not too surprised. She suspected the strain of business had contributed to her father's death. His company went into bankruptcy, as the solemn old Mr. Wilson had predicted it would, just a month after his death.

One of the S.C. North companies had taken over the housing project and, as far as Judith knew, was now making money on it. All that she and her mother were left with were the fine old house on Mount Pleasant, a small summer place at Millidgeville and the relatively small amount of insurance owned by Wilfred Barnes. There was no question of Judith continuing college until she earned her degree. She was forced to look for a job at once. And because there had been none that paid well enough in Port Winter, she'd gone to work for an insurance company in Manchester. However, her mother complained of being left in the big house in Port Winter, and so Judith had tried to find a job in her home town once again.

It was during Easter holidays the previous year that she'd met Alan Fraser at a dance given by the Yacht Club and he'd told her he was looking for a secretary. He was already chairman of the bridge authority and had a lot of extra paper work to be looked after. Because she liked Alan so much and thought the job might be a challenge, Judith eagerly offered herself for the post.

Now, as she emerged from the elevator, she found it hard to believe that so many months had passed. She was now firmly established in the job and knew most of the local personalities with whom Alan had to deal in charting the troubled course of the bridge. The offices which she and the young man shared were set apart from those occupied by his father, Brandon Fraser, and his partners. But they were on the same floor.

Judith reached in her purse and produced the office key. Up until the time Alan Fraser had been given the important job of spearheading the bridge construction, he had been a relatively minor cog in his father's office. This was not due in any way to a lack of ability on Alan's part but reflected a strained situation that existed between the quiet young man and his patrician father.

Judith sighed as she put aside her purse, seated herself at the typewriter desk in the outer office and began to sort her notes preparatory to putting Alan's letters into official form. There had been a time when she'd secretly hoped there might be a romance between herself and Alan. All during her growing-up days she'd worshipped him with the warmth of a younger sister. A smile crossed her lovely face. She must have acted the sisterly role too well, for that was how Alan always seemed to have thought of her. So even though she knew him and his problem better than most people, she had ended as being merely his secretary while he'd gotten himself engaged to a more flamboyant type.

She paused in her examination of the shorthand notes to decide if the description flamboyant was suitable to Alan's fiancée and decided that it was. Pauline Walsh was a striking blonde, a member of their own social set who had been divorced and was now living at home with her father, a wealthy owner of a shoe manufacturing plant. After a couple of years in New York, Pauline had come back to Port Winter to cut a dash.

As an occupation she had opened an art gallery, the first commercial one Port Winter had known, and stocked it with the work of local artists, along with a lot of reproductions of the better sort and a line of art supplies and high class stationery. Because she was outgoing and aggressive, she had done well.

Judith began typing the first of the letters:

21

a reply to one of the contractors who was building the road approaches on the eastern side of the harbor, explaining when the work would have to be completed.

She was half done with this when the phone rang. A hearty voice at the other end of the line inquired for Alan. Recognizing the voice, she asked pleasantly, "Is that you, Mayor Devlin?"

"Who else?" the Mayor said breezily. "How is my favorite girl today? When are you going to give up slaving for Alan and come work for me?"

She laughed. "I feel so secure here. You might not get elected next time. Then what would happen to me?"

"Smart girl," the Mayor agreed. "I may not even offer next time." He was one of Judith's favorite persons: a brash, middle-aged sports announcer with the local television station, who had made a host of friends with his nightly telecasts. When he had run for councilman as an amusing experience, he'd done so well he'd been persuaded to run for Mayor in the next election. His down-to-earth personality and innate honesty had won him the chief office in Port City.

"Is there any special message for Mr. Fraser?" she asked.

Mayor Jim Devlin chuckled. "Well, now, that's what I call a formal question!"

"He should be in at five," she said politely.

"No good for me; I've got a meeting to attend," the Mayor said. "But you can give him a message from me. And have him call me back here in the morning."

"Of course," she said.

"Tell him I think something's brewing," the Mayor went on. "Senator Lafferty and a committee from the North End Real Estate Owners Association have asked to be allowed to present a petition at the city council meeting tomorrow night."

"I see," she said, writing it down. "I understand the Senator has been out to look at the bridge several times recently."

"Doesn't surprise me," the Mayor said. "I don't know what it's all about, but I'd be willing to bet it's something unpleasant. This group have hired Lafferty as their legal representative. But I wouldn't be startled to find out that the bills went to S.C. North eventually."

Judith's voice expressed concern as she spoke into the phone. "You don't think he's still trying to do something to stop the bridge?"

"I don't see how that's possible," the

23

Mayor said, "not with the State and Federal governments having money in it, as well as the city. But he's a big man and might be interested in trying something. Tell Alan what's going on and have him phone me after nine in the morning."

"I will," Judith promised. "Thanks for calling."

"A pleasure," the Mayor told her in his best breezy sports announcer fashion. "It gives me a chance to talk to you." And he hung up on this happy note.

CHAPTER TWO

Judith worked on, and by the time Alan arrived back in the office at a few minutes before five she was typing the last of the letters he had left with her. She saw at a glance that his interview with Harvey Wheaton must have been a trying one. He looked weary.

Pausing before her desk, he asked, "What's been going on?"

"I've finished all your letters," Judith said. "And there was a phone call from Mayor Devlin."

Alan's thin face became grave. "What did he want?"

"He says Senator Lafferty is appearing before the City Council tomorrow night with representatives from the North End Real Estate Owners Association. He doesn't know what it's all about but thought you should be told. And he wants you to ring him in the morning, as soon after nine as you can."

The young lawyer offered her a tired smile. "Well, that fits in with Lafferty's being over to look at the bridge. He's got something on the frying pan, and no doubt the flame is being supplied by S.C. North."

Judith returned his smile. "It sounds as if they haven't given up their wrangling about the bridge yet. What's the matter with North? Is he so big he can't tolerate the idea of a fair defeat?"

"It's the loss of the steel contract that really made him livid," Alan said. "And I have an idea he's delighted to know we're hung up for steel now."

"How did you manage with Harvey Wheaton?"

Alan Fraser shrugged. "He put a long distance call through to the factory while I was there. They've been having some union troubles, but the shipment is on its way here."

"Then it may come in time to avoid a stoppage on the job," she said hopefully.

"There's a bare chance of it," he agreed. "But I don't count on any of their promises any more." He started for his office. "Bring the letters in and I'll sign them."

Judith gathered up the various letters and took them into the larger office occupied by Alan. Two of its walls were lined with law books. On the wall opposite his desk were his framed diploma, a large photo of himself along with other members of the Dartmouth track team, and several old English prints. Behind the large desk at which he was seated two tall old-fashioned windows looked out on King Street and the front of the North Building.

As Judith stood waiting, he carelessly glanced over the letters and affixed his signature to each of them. Then, gathering them, he passed them back to her.

Before she could leave he said, "I'd like to send a long letter to Wheaton's head office, trying to make clear our situation here and explain why any further delays in shipments could spell important trouble for us. Would you mind staying until six to get it done?"

Judith shook her head. "No. I'd be glad to stay."

Alan offered her a grateful smile. "Then that's what we'll do. I'll try to figure out a rough draft first. And then when we're finished we can go across to the Harbor Restaurant for dinner. My bonus to you for overtime."

She laughed lightly. "No bonus is required."

"I'd like to do it," he insisted. "Phone your mother and tell her you won't be home until after dinner and not to wait for you."

Judith hesitated. "I'm afraid any variation in the routine upsets her," she said. "Perhaps I should go home as soon as we've finished."

"Nonsense!" he said. "You should get out for dinner once in a while. This gives me a chance to treat you on my expense account. Go ahead; call her!"

Judith said, "I'll call and see if she's gone to any special trouble for dinner. If not, I'll stay in the city with you."

"That's more like it," Alan said approvingly.

Before Judith could leave the inner office, the door to the suite opened and Brandon Fraser came in. Alan's father was a tall, elegant man with iron-gray hair and the finely chiseled features of a patrician.

Advancing to the doorway of Alan's office, he gave Judith a nod and then focused his attention on his son. His dark soft hat and neat blue suit were in keeping with his dignified figure, and he carried a trench coat over his arm.

"I'm stopping by the Federal Club for a drink," he said in his voice of quiet authority. "Are you planning to visit there, or are you going straight home?"

Alan was on his feet. "I don't think I'll bother with the Club tonight, Dad. I have an important letter to get out."

His father's eyebrows raised ever so

slightly. "You'll be working late, then?"

"Yes. And I'll be having dinner across the street."

"I see," the older man said. His shrewd eyes gave Alan a piercing glance. "You're not in any sort of trouble with the bridge?"

"Just the regular day to day problems," Alan said.

"Oh!" His father hesitated in the doorway, not seeming quite convinced by Alan's answer. "Things are going ahead as you hoped, then?"

"I'd say so," was Alan's cool reply.

"Good," Brandon Fraser said. "Today marked the halfway point in getting the steel spans across the harbor, as I understand it?"

"We're halfway there," Alan agreed with a faint smile, "in spite of S.C. North."

His father frowned. "I think you should avoid thinking of this as a personal feud between you and S.C. North. I'm certain he doesn't consider it that."

Alan smiled sourly. "I fully agree. He sees me in conflict with his hired hands, such as Senator Lafferty."

Brandon Fraser's displeasure increased on hearing this remark. "I don't think you should be flippant about this business. Your appointment as chairman of the bridge authority is the most important one you've ever held. It is vital to your future that you make a success of it. And to do that you must weld the various fractions in the community into a harmonious team determined to make the project a success. And you can't hope for a successful completion without the backing of S.C. North and his interests."

"So it seems," Alan said quietly.

"It's your problem, of course," his father said in a grumpy voice, and looked down. "I'll let your mother know you won't be home until later." He gave Judith another brief nod, then turned and walked slowly out, closing the door to the corridor after him.

Alan gave her a rueful smile. "You have just heard me being put nicely in my place. You put those letters in envelopes ready to mail while I'm working on the draft of the one to the steel factory."

Judith went back to her own office, feeling sorry for the young man. It was not the first time she'd heard his father rebuke him, and she was certain it wouldn't be the last. There was a strange relationship between Alan Fraser and his father. It dated back to the death of Alan's older brother, Brian, a few years earlier. Brian had been his father's favorite, and Brandon Fraser had been shattered when Brian was killed by a stray bullet in a hunting mishap.

With a sigh she placed the last of the letters in its envelope and prepared to return to the inner office and take down the message Alan was preparing for the steel company. Before joining him again, she quickly dialed her home phone number and spoke with her mother for a few minutes. At first Millicent seemed peevish at the idea of her remaining in the city for dinner, but she did admit there had been no special meal prepared, and when she found Judith was planning to dine with Alan Fraser she dropped all her objections, merely plaintively requesting that her daughter not be too late returning. Judith wearily promised she wouldn't be and hung up.

Alan was absorbed in his task of preparing the letter when she went in. He gave her a brief glance. "This is not coming easily," he said. "I want to be sure to get the main points over strongly." And he nodded for her to sit and wait until he was ready to dictate.

It was nearly six-thirty when she finished typing the completed letter. By that time Alan was standing waiting for her. He smiled as she addressed the envelope.

"We'll want it to go special delivery," he

said. "Probably won't get there any quicker, but at least they'll know we wanted them to get it in a hurry." He paused. "Hungry?"

"Starving," she admitted as she sealed the letter in its long envelope and got up to get her coat and join him.

"I'll go ahead," he volunteered, "and while I'm mailing these, you can freshen up for dinner."

Judith smiled. "Thanks," she said. "That would help. I feel a wreck after being here all day. I'm not sure this suit is right for the Harbor Room."

"You look great," he said gallantly. "Don't worry about it."

A brief stop in the washroom and fresh make-up gave her some confidence. The suit was neatly tailored and did fit her well. She met him in the downstairs lobby with a smile.

Alan said, "I'm looking forward to dinner. One of S.C. North's few projects of which I approve is the Harbor Room. It offers a decent meal, and the view is superb."

She laughed. "I doubt that he enjoys it any more now that the bridge is going up."

"You may have a point there," he agreed as he held the door open for her to go out into the street.

They waited for the lights to change and

then hurried across to the tall, recently constructed North Building. One of the express elevators serving the penthouse restaurant opened its doors, and they stepped inside to be whisked to the top.

The headwaiter greeted them as soon as they left the elevator for the carpeted, glass-walled luxury of the Harbor Room. The big roof-top restaurant was doing a brisk business, but because of its unusually spacious design and carefully spaced tables it had an air of quiet decorum. They were seated at one of the round, white-clothed tables near the outside glass wall, with a commanding view of the harbor and the rapidly rising bridge. The headwaiter made a smiling comment and then left them with oversize menus to select their choice of dinners.

They decided on lobster dinners, since the Harbor Room was noted for its sea food. Their dinners ordered, they sat back to talk and relax as the day drew to an end.

Alan's thin young face was more serious than usual. "I had the idea Harvey Wheaton might have heard something when I talked to him today," he said. "And the Mayor certainly had news. Also, I'm not altogether sure but that Dad has heard some rumors there is trouble in the offing."

"You really feel that?"

"I'm afraid so," he said. "Perhaps after I talk with the Mayor in the morning I should phone the Governor in Concord and see if any of the gossip has reached his august ears."

Judith pictured the granite-faced, middle-aged man who headed the state and whose irascible temper and urgent desire not to be bothered by civic feuds were legendary. She said, "It's not likely he'll want to hear anything about it."

"But extremely likely that he has, if Senator Lafferty is mixed up in what's happening. When Lafferty was a Senator, he and the Governor served the same party side by side, and they're close personal friends."

"I suppose that's what makes Lafferty so useful to S.C. North," Judith suggested with some bitterness.

"That's easy to figure," he agreed. "I won't bother Governor Thorne unless I feel I have to. But he does have a big stake in the bridge. The state has more cash behind the project than the city; the federal government is merely backing the state's borrowing for the project. So in the end it is the Governor who is chiefly responsible."

"I see what you mean," she said.

"Technically, the bridge authority has the

full say now," Alan went on. "And as chairman, I should be the ruler of the roost. But it doesn't work out quite that simply. We still have to deal with politicians and politics all the way until the last bolt is fixed in place."

Judith gave him an understanding look. "I think that is what worries your father. He knows what a hard position you're in."

Alan looked amused. "What worries my father is his complete lack of confidence in me!"

"Is that really true?"

"I think so."

"And I doubt it. He worries about you. But I'm sure he's secretly proud of what you've done so far."

"The only person he was ever truly proud of was Brian," the young man opposite her said bitterly. "You must know that! You grew up with us. It was always Brian who was the favorite."

Judith tried to placate him, saying, "But isn't it true the older son is usually the favorite?"

"Not necessarily," Alan said stubbornly. "Everything that Brian did was right, and almost everything I tried was wrong. Father's been stupidly one-sided in his attitude."

"You're winning him over," she assured him.

Alan glanced out at the harbor and the partially finished bridge; the gray light of a gathering dusk served as a background for the horizon of the old city. "I wonder," he mused. "Perhaps if I work a miracle and the bridge finally becomes a reality." He glanced across at her. "You can't have any idea how many times the bridge has been proposed and the project abandoned because of petty greed and jealousies. Now North wants to start trouble again!"

"But you've gone so far with it!"

"Don't fool yourself that means it will be completed," Alan warned her. "Nothing would please North and his cronies better than to see it abandoned and the girders rusting without ever having carried a traffic load."

She smiled confidently. "They won't stop you now!"

"Well, at least that's a nice note to begin dinner with," he observed with a smile as the waiter came up to their table with his loaded serving tray. The food was delicious, and for some time they gave their attention to it. When they picked up the conversation again, it turned to more personal matters.

Alan touched a napkin to his mouth. "We

should do this more often," he said. "After all, we are old friends, and we have hardly any chance really to talk at the office."

Judith tilted her head slightly in a demure smile. "Do you think Pauline would approve?"

At the mention of the striking blonde divorcee to whom Alan had become engaged, he looked embarrassed. He said, "I don't see why she should object. After all, she has her own friends. I'm sure when she goes to New York on buying trips, such as the one she's on now, she must meet many of her old friends."

"And you wouldn't object to her having dinner with any of the male ones?"

He shrugged. "She dines with her ex-husband occasionally."

"That's different," she said. "You know there is no romantic interest there any longer. I mean other male friends she knew before coming back here."

Alan leaned forward in his chair earnestly. "Look, one bad marriage has taught Pauline at least a single truth. If there isn't trust between two people, there's nothing. We're not narrow in our outlooks. I expect her to continue having her friends, and I'll have mine."

"I know Pauline is very modern in her

ideas as well as her artistic tastes." Judith smiled. "I only hope they both turn out to be sound."

"She's doing great with her gallery. Her father financed it, never expecting to get a penny back, and she's been making a nice profit."

"I know," Judith admitted. "Pauline is a wonder."

He smiled. "She is. And she's determined not to make the same errors she made in her first marriage."

"Understandable," Judith said. "And just in case she might see me as an error, I think we should be discreet. I'd like to keep my job, and your wife-to-be might have a different idea if she discovered we went out dining together regularly."

The organist who played in the Harbor Room in the evenings had taken his place and started to play soft pleasant mood music in the background. The myriad of tiny light bulbs fixed in large clusters in a number of overhead spots gave the suggestion of distant stars. It made a truly romantic setting, and Judith could just barely catch the vexed expression on Alan's face across the table.

He said, "You know I sometimes wonder what happened to us."

She smiled. "Happened to us?"

Alan nodded. "Yes. We went around together as youngsters and in high school. It would have been logical if we'd gone on dating. Why didn't we?"

She shrugged. "I couldn't tell you. Perhaps because you went away to college. You were at Dartmouth and I went to Durham. We made different friends."

"And when I came home on holidays, I found you were seeing Brian for an occasional date," he reminded her.

"Brian and I had grown up together, too," she said, "even though he was a little older."

"I suppose I got jealous. I always steered clear of Brian's girls."

"But I wasn't really Brian's girl! We didn't have more than four or five dates altogether."

He smiled sadly. "That would have been enough to keep me away from you in those days. I avoided any competition with Brian."

"So that's why you stopped asking me to go anywhere?"

"I'm afraid so," he admitted. "I can see it was wrong now."

"Perhaps not," she said, looking down. "You've found Pauline. She's a beautiful girl."

"Sure," he said quietly. "But then so are you."

Judith was thankful for the dimness of the room, since it prevented him from seeing her blush. She said, "Times change, Alan. I'm quite happy to be your secretary now. I'm not the rich little miss I was a few years ago."

"Money hasn't anything to do with it."

"I think it has," she argued. "Two people in a town like this should be of the same background if they plan to marry. Otherwise they open themselves to a lot of criticism."

"Your social position is as good as mine or better," Alan pointed out. "Your mother comes from one of the oldest families in town. You'll find the Melrose name on half the historical plates."

She laughed. "But I don't even have the Melrose name. My father was an ordinary Barnes. And we don't have any money left at all. Just the house, if we can manage to keep that."

"So?"

"If I married anyone in Port Winter with money, I'd be accused of fortune hunting," Judith said. "Thank you. I'm happier as a secretary."

Alan gave her a penetrating glance.

"What about Miles Estey?"

Again she blushed and looked down. In a low voice she said, "That's over."

"I'd hope so, for your sake," Alan told her. "But are you sure?"

"Very sure."

"Have you heard from him since he left here?"

She still avoided Alan's eyes. "I had several letters."

"Lately?"

"No."

"I never felt he was right for you," Alan said earnestly.

"Would you be a fair judge?" she asked, finally looking at him.

He hesitated before replying; then he said, "Frankly, I suppose not." There was a moment of silence. Then, somewhat awkwardly, he said, "I suppose we'd better go."

"Yes," she agreed. "I think we should."

CHAPTER THREE

Darkness had fallen by the time he drove her home. They went up King Street and around the park, which was bounded by central business streets on all but one side. Here were congregated the city's chief theatres and largest hotel, along with several of the more popular restaurants and shops. As usual, the streets were busy at this time of night.

"How much the city is changing," she said, glancing out her side window at the old burial ground that dated to Revolutionary Days.

"We have to change with it," he reminded her from the wheel.

"In many ways I find that somewhat sad," she said. "I liked Port Winter as it was."

His lean face was illuminated by the faint light from the dash so that she saw his smile. "You were always sentimental! I remember that once you had a sad time when your mother wanted to give one of your favorite dolls to a charity."

She laughed. "Don't remind me! I'd forgotten! I was heartbroken!"

"As I say, you always had a strong streak of nostalgia."

They drove past a rather hideous auto clinic covering several blocks of what she remembered as a pleasant residential district. "Don't tell me that monstrosity is an improvement," she said, indicating it with a nod.

Alan gave it a brief glance. "I think Dad negotiated the properties for the deal. The builders expect to make a lot of money."

She settled back against the seat with a sigh. "A lot of money! That's all that seems to count! Any horror is endured if it means someone is going to make a lot of money! So we have the fumes from the pulp mills, the oil refineries and the steel mills, all in the pious name of S.C. North."

He laughed. "A truly Spartan character. They tell me he doesn't even smoke."

"I don't wonder," she exclaimed. "Not after the way he's polluted the local air. He knows it's dangerous enough breathed straight!"

They went down a steep hill and then made a sharp right and drove up an equally steep grade that led to the fashionable Mount Pleasant district. From this area there was an unrestricted view of the city, and when the new bridge was completed a separate roadway would make this part of Port Winter much more accessible. The fine houses built in the neighborhood over the years bordered on the Port Winter Public Gardens and Lake. Indeed, on a fine afternoon Judith often went there for a stroll.

Judith's home was located on rocks above the level of the street. A fairly imposing total of concrete steps led up to the cottage, and they were often treacherously icy in winter. Since her father's death they had been able to pay out little for upkeep of the property, so the gray-shingled cottage with its quaint white shutters was showing some signs of neglect. Prominent among them were the cracked and broken steps that cried out for repair every time she went up and down them.

Now, as Alan saw her to the door, she apologized for their condition. "We just don't seem to get around to repairs," she said.

He held her lightly by the arm. "Dad has a good handyman," he said. "I'll have him come over some day."

"Don't without checking with me," Judith begged. "You know how odd Mother is about having people around when I'm not here. She has an obsession that we're going to be robbed by some stranger, though what they'd find worth taking I'm sure I don't know," she ended breathlessly as they were at the top of the steps.

Alan smiled at her. "It's been a pleasant evening. We ought to work overtime more often."

Judith regarded him with a twinkle in her eyes. "I've tried to warn you of possible consequences."

"Hang possible consequences," he said, still standing there admiring her. "I'm really able to talk to you. Pauline doesn't take an interest in anything but her own affairs and the gallery. She pretends she doesn't understand when I talk about the bridge."

"Perhaps she doesn't."

"She could make it her business to learn more about it."

Judith smiled. "Then she'd bore you by talking about the same thing you live with every day. I don't think there's any pleasing you!"

"You do very well," Alan said quietly. And without any warning he reached and took her in his arms for a lasting kiss.

"Well!" she said in a startled tone as he let her go.

"It's been a long time," he said quietly.

"And it really shouldn't have happened at all."

He smiled. "I'm not sorry. What about you?"

Again she was glad of the protecting darkness. "Don't ask me!" she said quietly. And then, "Good night, Alan."

"Good night, Judith," he said with warmth. "It was truly a good evening, and don't let your conscience bother you."

She made no reply but unlocked the door and went inside. A moment later she watched as he went down the steps to his car. From the living room came the sound of a television drama, with dramatic cries, the sound of running and outbursts of pistol fire. Then she heard it snapped off, and her mother appeared in the living room doorway to greet her.

"Well, darling, so you're finally home!" Millicent Barnes said. "Did you have a good evening?"

"Dinner was good," Judith said. "Alan felt he owed it to me because I worked late. Of course he really didn't."

Her mother was wearing one of the faded dressing gowns that seemed to match her own ruined beauty. She was painfully thin and had the gown tied tightly about her. Now her worn face showed a sly smile.

"You don't have to be coy with me, darling," she said with meaning. "I slipped away from the television a moment and watched you through the curtain at the window."

"Mother! How could you!"

Millicent raised a thin hand. "You don't have to hide things from your own mother," she protested in a voice overly sweet with understanding. "I'm just so happy for you!"

"What do you mean?" Judith asked suspiciously.

Her mother clasped her hands at her waist and made strange little movements with her lips before she spoke. "Well, if I must say it, I saw you in Alan's arms. I don't mind telling you it's what I've been hoping for, only I didn't think you had the sense to let it happen!"

Judith's pretty face shamed with ashamed astonishment. "Mother, how can you say such a thing!"

"Well, it's true," Millicent went on in her drab, trembling voice. "I have prayed that Alan Fraser would fall in love with you and we'd be able to hold up our heads in this town again."

"Look," Judith said helplessly, "you're getting this all wrong."

"You can be frank with me," Millicent said. "I won't let on to anyone you two are going to be engaged. A mother has the right to know first!"

"We are not engaged!" Judith said angrily. "If you recall, Alan is engaged to Pauline Walsh!"

Her mother's lips quivered. "But I supposed he'd broken that."

"He hasn't!"

"But I saw him kissing you just now!"

"Mother!" Judith said reprovingly. "That didn't mean anything!"

"Didn't mean anything!" Millicent Barnes echoed, her voice becoming very high-pitched.

"No!"

"Then what kind of a way was that to be acting?" Her mother was angry in her disappointment.

"What did you mean by spying on us?" Judith wanted to know.

"A mother has the right to watch over her own!"

"Let me say you've nicely twisted that to your own convenience," Judith said, angry herself now. "I won't put up with your prying. I warn you!"

"To think you'd make yourself cheap in the eyes of a man like Alan," her mother wailed. "No wonder no decent fellow will take an interest in you, and you wind up with somebody like that awful Miles Estey!"

"Leave Miles out of this!" Judith said sharply.

"A thief!" her mother cried indignantly. "That's what he was! And if he hadn't slunk out of town, you'd probably have decided you should marry him!"

"Perhaps I would have," Judith said grimly between her teeth.

"You're reckless and wild, just like your father before you!" Millicent went on, going into high on a favorite subject. "My parents warned me not to marry him, but I wouldn't listen! And I've lived to rue the day! And then when I think you've done something to help us, you let me down just as your father did!"

Judith took a few steps toward her own room and then turned to warn the weeping woman, "Mother, I'm telling you if you don't stop this kind of nonsense, I'm going back to that job in Manchester again."

"You'd do anything to torment me!" Millicent sobbed.

"I'd do anything to keep you from peeking out windows and poking your silly nose into my affairs," Judith said grimly. "Good night, Mother! Thank you for watching over me!" She strode into her own room and slammed the door after her.

So often had Millicent behaved stupidly

and bungled things for them both that Judith had lost patience with her. It had been Millicent's pathetic attempts to push her in a social circle that no longer was interested in them that had made Judith certain she must find new friends and a new life in another group. And it was this decision that had led her to falling in love with Miles Estey.

She'd met Miles at a party one night and thought him one of the nicer young men who were newcomers in town.

"I'm a wrong-side-of-the-tracks kind of guy," he'd been frank to tell her with a smile on his friendly, freckled face. "And from what I hear, you're entitled to a high rating in local society. One of the debs who live up on the hill."

"I've come down a mite," she told him jokingly as they stood in a corner of the crowded, noisy room. "My family have lost their money."

Miles was tall and red-haired, with careless good looks and disturbingly clear blue eyes. Those eyes now searched hers as he said quietly, "You've got real class and that's something you won't ever lose."

"Thanks!" she bantered. "Now I won't worry about getting it insured."

He continued to stare at her. "You are

also the first good reason I've found for re-maining in this silly old New Hampshire town."

Judith raised her eyebrows. "Didn't you come here to take a job?"

"I can find a job anywhere."

She laughed. "You're lucky."

"I mean it," he said seriously. "As I told you, I come from the wrong side of the tracks in a small Rhode Island town. But I learned one thing early. You can make it in this country if you've got a few natural brains and a little education. So that's how I happen to be an accountant."

"And you're going to work for S.C. North, aren't you?"

He gave her a mocking smile. "Doesn't just about everyone in this town work for North or some company owned by him?"

She sighed. "It's getting to be the truth. I wish it weren't. He's too powerful."

"Smart girl!" Miles glanced around the room. "You know the old saw about absolute power corrupting absolutely. It's true. And it is happening here. Pretty near every-one in this room gets his living money from the great North, and they'd all be in a panic if you asked them to say honestly what they think about his policies."

"How about you?"

He smiled. "Not me. I'm a free agent. That's why I'm not apt to be popular in this town."

"What kind of job have you taken?"

The red-haired giant winked at her. "I'm an executive," he said. "You don't expect an up-and-coming young man like me to settle for anything but an executive position!"

She smiled. "I should have known better."

"I'm to be chief assistant to Charles North," Miles said proudly.

Her eyebrows rose. "The great man's youngest son!"

"Correct!" Miles went on. "I'm looking after the timber division under him. It's a pretty important part of the whole operation. We buy lumber land as well as look after pulp for the mill."

"I wish you luck," she said. "I'm sure you'll do well."

"Just by meeting you I'm doing fine," he assured her in his intense way.

And it had seemed that he was headed for a fine future in Port Winter. Judith began dating him regularly. They made a happy combination, and it seemed likely that Miles might ask her to marry him.

Then the shadow had fallen on him. It

happened overnight. Suddenly there were ugly rumors making the rounds of Port City that larceny had taken place in the offices of the North Timber Division. Books had been fixed, entries forged, and large amounts of cash were missing. Miles didn't mention it to Judith for a while. But she saw a change in him and knew that he was badly upset.

Two weeks passed before he brought it out in the open. He was bitter and defeated. "A lot of money has been stolen from the company, Judith," he said. "And I've been tagged as the thief."

"But you didn't!" she protested, certain it wasn't possible.

He smiled bitterly. "I've tried to prove that, but Charles North is as slick as his father. He's fixed it neatly so that I'm the only possible suspect, although I know he took the money. But nobody in this town figures a North would rob himself."

Judith stared at him in dismay. "What are you going to do?"

"I've been given two choices."

From his tone she inferred they must offer no solution, but she asked, "What are they?"

"Charles North is willing to plead my case with his father because I have been so competent and such a good friend to him. He feels sure he can persuade the old man to let me go free if I'll leave town at once." Miles gave her a meaningful glance. "You can see through that, can't you? Charles wants me openly to acknowledge guilt. That way he's in the clear. Maybe he even figures his father knows he took the money. But he'll be safe."

"But it's no good," she objected. "You should try to prove it wasn't you!"

"There just isn't any way to do that," Miles said unhappily. "That brings me to the alternate choice. I can face a court and take whatever sentence they hand out for what I'm supposed to have done."

"But surely you can prove your innocence in court."

"Not in a town where North owns everything and everyone. I won't get any kind of a fair hearing."

"There must be some answer," she fretted. "If you leave with everyone thinking you're guilty, you won't be able to make a fresh start."

"It won't be easy," he admitted. "But since the other choice is jail, it looks as if I'll have to take my chances."

Judith looked at him with incredulous eyes. "But our friends, everyone, they'll not understand. They'll think you really took the money!"

Miles' blue eyes flashed angrily. "My real friends won't think that!"

"I hope not," she said faintly.

"I'm not dragging you into it," he told her, taking her in his arms.

"And I surely intend to stand by you," she said. "You can make your mind up to that."

He hadn't argued, and the warmth of his embrace should have told her that this was the signal of a parting. He kissed her with a fierce, tormented passion and seemed reluctant to let her go. But when he had allowed her to be free of his arms, he had quickly left her.

Her next word from him was a letter mailed in Boston. He begged her forgiveness and said he was trying to make a fresh start. He promised he would write again. His second letter came some time after she had gone to Manchester to work and was forwarded to her. His tone was less optimistic, and he was frank in telling her that no one seemed to want to trust him with a responsible job. The Norths had spread their venom about him well. The last time she heard from him he'd merely sent a Christmas greeting with his name and no message or forwarding address.

By the time Judith returned to Port Winter, the theft and Miles Estey had been pushed aside for other more immediate matters of local gossip. The new bridge was the center of attention, and with it Alan Fraser had stepped into the local limelight. No one mentioned Miles to Judith, but she knew many of her friends must think about him when they met her. She made a point of not mentioning his name, either. But there were times, such as now, when he was very much in her mind.

She often asked herself if she had truly been in love with him.

She turned down the coverlet and began slowly to prepare for bed. It had been typical of her mother to spy on her and mistake the innocent kiss she had exchanged with Alan Fraser for the sign of a great romance. No use attempting to explain to her any more than she had just tried to do.

As she slipped between the sheets and turned off the lights, she recalled a conversation she'd had with the handsome Brian on one of their several dates.

She had said, "You're so much more aggressive than Alan."

Alan's older brother had flashed her one of his winning smiles. "You really think so?"

"Yes. It's one of the first things I noticed about you."

"Alan has plenty of ability," Brian told her, "probably more than I have. But he lacks confidence."

"I feel that," she agreed.

Brian had become serious. "Father takes it for granted that I should do everything better than Alan; sometimes I find that isn't so easy. And it also isn't good for Alan."

She'd smiled. "You think he has a younger brother complex?"

"Very much so." Brian nodded. "Father is making it worse. He wants me to go into the firm with him, and he feels Alan should go to another city if he wants to practice law."

"That doesn't seem fair," she said, "especially as Alan probably wants to join your father's firm."

"He does," Brian said. "And he hasn't any idea how Father feels about him as yet. I've got to talk to Dad and somehow try to make him change his mind."

Judith had been impressed by Brian's generosity. "You'll not lose anything by doing it, I'm sure," she'd said. "And I'm glad I've gotten to know you. Somehow it makes me able to understand Alan and his problems better."

He had given her a troubled glance. "I've enjoyed having you as a friend, too," he said. "I only hope Alan takes it the right way."

She'd shown surprise. "Why should he object to our being friends?"

Brian had shrugged. "That's hard to explain. Alan sometimes gets queer ideas. He's moody, you know. There is a kind of weak streak in his nature, a tendency to give up when he comes face to face with a situation he doesn't understand. In a way, I suppose Father may not be entirely wrong about him."

"Meaning?"

"He has too many warring elements in his nature," Brian said. "And he's far too sensitive for his own good. Faced with a true crisis, I'm not sure that he wouldn't break."

Judith stared up into the darkness. Those words rang anew in her ears, although they'd been uttered by Alan's now dead brother on a night long ago. Surely the crisis had arrived for Alan! Would his brother's ominous prediction come true?

CHAPTER FOUR

Judith was positive they were facing trouble when their first caller the following morning was Councilman Fred Harvey. Councilman Harvey had been one of those supporting Alan for the post of chairman of the bridge authority, and she had always had a warm regard for the little man. Originally he had been brought to Port Winter to manage one of S.C. North's smaller enterprises. He had been clever enough to see the need for the service in the city and had left his job with North to establish a rival service of the same type.

His business had become a success overnight and, due to Fred Harvey's shrewd manipulations, he was soon an S.C. North in miniature, having his hand in a number of other firms. North eventually grudgingly acknowledged the little man's talents as a promoter by making a bid to buy the original service, which Fred Harvey gladly sold him at a neat profit, since he already had enough new enterprises to keep him busy.

The feud between Harvey and S.C. North was not an open one. It had never been declared. But each worked behind the scenes in his own way to harass the other. Judith had the opinion that was why Councilman Fred Harvey had worked so hard for Alan. He wanted to see him get the position as head of the bridge committee so S.C. North wouldn't get the steel contract for the construction job. Of course she couldn't prove that any more than S.C. North could, but Alan had been pledged to give the rival company represented by Harvey Wheaton the contract, and so it looked suspicious to her.

The amusing thing about Fred Harvey was that he was innocence itself in appearance and manner. A genial, slightly overweight man of small stature, he wore a perpetual smile on his broad face and beamed happily at the world through his heavy horn-rimmed glasses. His voice was high-pitched and rather unimpressive and further put his opponents off-guard. But there was nothing naïve about his alert mind, and perhaps the tipoff? to his keen brain was his direct logic in an argument. And his neat thinking habits were reflected in his dress. His clothes were tailored and of the most expensive materials, and he showed remarkably good taste in his choice of them.

As he presented himself before Judith on this morning in late May, he was hatless and wearing a light gray suit of an intricate tiny check pattern. His tie was a dark gray, the collar of his white shirt contoured to show his round face to the best advantage. His dark hair was slicked back, and his eyes beamed at her through his horn-rimmed glasses.

He smiled as he asked, "Alan here yet, Judy?"

She nodded. "Yes. He's on the phone with the Mayor at the moment." She was used to Councilman Harvey calling her Judy and didn't mind it from him.

The short man teetered back and forth on his heels. "That figures," he said with an air of inward amusement.

Judith gave him a searching glance. "We don't usually see you so early in the day."

"No, you don't!" He was still smiling and obviously enjoying her curiosity.

She knew him well enough to ask, "Something doing?"

Fred Harvey chuckled. "Always something doing in Port Winter! You ought to know that! This is the East's busiest little metropolis!"

Judith grimaced. "I've heard it described in other ways!"

"I saw you standing out on the bridge yesterday," he said. "You must be a brave girl."

Judith smiled. "Alan led me out there and left me. I was too frightened to move."

"No wonder," Fred Harvey said. "It's a long way down to the water. Alan should be more careful of you. I would be."

"I can imagine," she observed dryly, sliding a sheet of paper into her typewriter.

The Councilman strolled jauntily across to the single window of the outer office with its view of the alley. "Not very inspiring," was his comment as he peered out. Then he turned to her, still beaming. "Why don't you come work for me? I'll give you a good-sized office of your own and two big windows with a view of the park."

"Why must you always tempt me?" she mocked him. "And you so charming!"

Going along with the joke, he chuckled again. "The fact I'm practically irresistible has nothing to do with it."

The door to the inner office opened and Alan came out. With a grim smile he said, "I didn't know you were out here."

"I believe in getting my day started early. How's the Mayor?" the Councilman said in a teasing manner.

"Just bringing me up to date on a few things," Alan said. "What do you know?"

"Probably not much that the Mayor hasn't told you," Harvey was willing to concede.

Alan frowned. "Don't tell me you called just to pay your compliments to Judith!"

Fred Harvey laughed. "Well, Judy is always worth a visit. You've got a gem in this girl, and you don't appreciate her." He gestured toward her with a pudgy hand.

"Quit stalling!" Alan protested. "What's doing with Senator Lafferty?"

For the first time Fred Harvey dropped his smile. Giving Alan a wise look, he said, "If you're planning to cross the harbor on that bridge of yours, I'd advise you to equip yourself with a pair of water-wings."

"What are you saying?" Alan asked.

"The Senator is out to make trouble, Alan," the little man warned him.

Alan stood there with an expression of scorn on his face and his hands thrust in his trousers pockets. "The Senator is always looking for trouble one way or another, and often he's the one who lands in the trouble."

Fred Harvey grinned. "The Mayor tell you what's going on?"

"He said this group from the North End Real Estate Owners Association is having the Senator present a petition for them tonight. He hasn't any idea what it's about. What do you know about the association?"

"It's legitimate enough," Fred Harvey admitted. "But it doesn't have many members, and most of them are also big shots in the Democratic Club and friends of the Senator."

Alan nodded. "So he's using them as a front?"

"Could be."

"What's he after?"

The Councilman looked wise. "What's S.C. North after?"

"My scalp, among other things," Alan said. His eyes narrowed with real concern as he asked, "You think at this late date North has put the Senator up to new obstructionist tactics to try and delay finishing the bridge?"

"That's why I'm here this morning," the stout little Councilman admitted. "I was the one most responsible for your appointment. I figure I've gotten you in this mess; the least I can do is stand by you."

"Thanks," Alan said bitterly. "Then you actually think this amounts to something?"

Fred Harvey beamed happily again. "When S.C. North and the Senator put their heads together, they usually come up with something. I figure they've got a dilly this time."

"Oh?"

The Councilman nodded. "You remember when the plans for the bridge were first drawn up," he said. "There was a spur leading directly to Harrigan Street and on to the shopping plaza in the North End and the residential area beyond."

Alan gave Judith a quick glance as he considered this. Then he told Fred Harvey, "Yes. I believe we did consider an extra exit leading to Harrigan Street. We abandoned the idea because the cost was out of all proportion to the service the spur would offer."

"Some people don't see it that way."

"What about it?" Alan wanted to know. "When we changed our plans, no one protested."

Fred Harvey gave him a crafty look. "That was because the Senator was having his annual Florida vacation at the time. Now that the omission has been brought to his attention by the North End Real Estate Owners Association, he's on the warpath."

"But that's ridiculous!" Alan protested. "The plans were approved months ago."

"Ridiculous or not," Harvey said, "the Senator is going to ask you to halt work on the bridge until the question of a spur to the North End has been thoroughly gone into."

Alan drew his hands out of his pockets and stared at the little man in complete amazement. "Halt work on the bridge!"

"That's it!"

"But it doesn't make sense," Alan said. "We've already received our grants from the state and federal governments, and they don't include the expense of that spur. Added to that, the cost of a delay would be ruinous whether we decided to go ahead with the spur or not. It could add millions to the construction costs of the bridge."

"The Senator knows that," Harvey said calmly.

"Then he's deliberately trying to scuttle the entire project," Alan said angrily, "even though it's half completed!"

"From his point of view and S.C. North's, it makes sense," Harvey told him.

"The public won't stand for it," Alan said.

"North owns both newspapers in town," Harvey reminded him. "He can mold public opinion pretty much as he likes."

"But this is too obvious," Alan said.

"Maybe and maybe not," Fred Harvey warned him. "I think I can tell you what they have in mind. They'll get the Mayor and Council to vote on a delay until the matter can be considered. Then it will be tossed in the lap of you and the bridge authority. You'll have a joint meeting with the Council, and no one will be able to agree. Meanwhile, with construction halted, your daily expenses will mount with nothing to show for it. When this has gone on long enough, the Senator will urge the Council to vote on abandonment of the project until a Governor's committee can review the entire matter and assess the practical advantages of a North End spur. By that time you will have resigned as chairman and North will be working to put one of his men in your position."

"You make it sound logical," Alan admitted.

"I know what's in the air," Fred Harvey assured him. "And it isn't the scent of roses! Once North has his key man in charge of the bridge authority, the Governor's committee will come to the conclusion the spur isn't necessary, and they'll start construction again. Only this time you won't have anything to say about it, and S.C. North will. And they'll use North steel to finish the job!"

"That's what it's all about!" Alan said.

"What else?" the Councilman wanted to know.

Alan couldn't seem to comprehend the situation even now that Fred Harvey had explained it to him in detail. "I can't believe they'd risk wrecking the project to get their own way," he said in a wondering tone.

"Then you don't know the Senator or S.C. North very well," the Councilman told him. "This represents a chance for a hefty profit into the bargain."

Alan gave him a troubled look. "What do you think I should do?"

The little man took time to give Judith a wink. "Surprise them," he said.

Alan's brow furrowed. "In what way?"

"They expect you to fight them."

"What else can I do?"

"Upset their plans by pretending to consider the petition," the Councilman suggested.

Alan showed bewilderment. "I don't see what good that will do. You've just finished explaining how they intend to proceed. And whether I oppose them or pretend to go along with them, it will result in the same thing — a delay!"

"Not if you're smooth enough handling it."

"I don't see how a delay can be avoided," Alan said, still frowning.

Fred Harvey shrugged. "If the worst came to the worst, you could go along with them, pretend to agree and keep on as chairman of the board. Let them take it to the Governor and have the state put up the extra money for the spur. You can still let them build the

North End spur and defeat the Senator and S.C. North by spoiling their main objective: to get you out of your job and North's steel into the construction of the bridge."

"It would be a shallow victory," Alan said grimly. "The bridge costs would skyrocket, and we'd be agreeing to something to which I'm completely opposed."

"Better than losing out altogether," the Councilman suggested.

Alan looked at him directly. "If I compromise, I won't be doing an honest job. And you're the one who appointed me."

Fred Harvey smiled. "All politics is compromise. You'll have to learn that if you're going anywhere."

"I guess I'm not good political material, then," Alan said.

"All you have to be for the time being is a good poker player," the little man advised. "Bluff them. Don't let them think you're willing to give way, but don't put yourself out on a limb, either. Stand pat while they do all the screaming."

"That won't be easy!"

Fred Harvey beamed at him. "You shouldn't expect it to be. But it's the first stage of the battle. Just sit pat! The Senator is hoping that as soon as the Council votes to halt work on the bridge, you'll give up."

Alan asked, "Is this the best service you can offer?"

"For now."

"If it's a sample of what you'll pass along later, I can do without it," Alan said. "I'll have to figure some way to halt those chiselers on my own."

The little man grinned at him. "You'll have a chance to. I'm going to Washington on business this afternoon. I'll be gone for the balance of the week."

Judith remembered the Councilman's refusal to use planes for his many jaunts to other parts of the country. Speaking up for the first time, she asked, "Will you be driving or going by train?"

"Driving to Boston and taking a train from there," the Councilman told her. "So I can't be back before Monday or Tuesday." He beamed at Alan. "Maybe by then you'll have a strategy of your own worked out."

"You only say that because you know I won't," Alan said sullenly. "I'd think you'd stay in town with this breaking!"

"More important things to look after," Fred Harvey assured him with a wise smile. And with a farewell nod to Judith, he said, "Don't forget that job is always open to you, Judy."

"The knowledge of it sustains me," Judy

70

told him in the same mocking manner.

"Good luck!" the Councilman said to Alan as the young lawyer saw him out.

"Thanks!" Alan said a shade too bitterly. When the Councilman had gone out, he closed the door after him and turned to give Judith a glance. "What do you say to that?"

"I'm not surprised," Judith said.

"I suppose I shouldn't be, either," he admitted, starting to pace back and forth in her office. "I should have known North wouldn't give up so easily."

"He rarely does."

"But what he has to gain in this case is not that great! I can't see him holding up the bridge just to win the contract for the rest of the steel."

"Isn't it more than that? A need to prove that he can have his own way in Port Winter?"

"I suppose so. He hates to be crossed."

"And this bridge business has been a reverse for him the whole town knows about," Judith pointed out. "He'll probably never rest easy until he has won the battle."

Alan gave her a surprised look. "You're not agreeing with Harvey that I should play along with North's crowd in this to keep my position?"

She shrugged. "I don't know enough

71

about it. But I would hate to see you resign."

"It may be all I'm honorably able to do," he said. "If Mayor Devlin can't dismiss this at the Council meeting, we're in the soup. Once the Council votes for a delay, the Senator has won the first round."

"Will the Council take the petition seriously?"

"That will depend on how many S.C. North supporters there are among the Councilmen," Alan said. "We know our side will lose one vote with Harvey away."

"Surely he could have stayed here another day," she said.

"No point in asking him. He had no intention of staying, and he'd only have refused me."

"Still, you weren't very polite in accepting his advice."

"That kind of advice! What did you expect me to say?" Alan demanded.

She smiled ruefully. "Of course it's up to you."

Alan smiled at her apologetically. "Sorry. I didn't mean to put you on the griddle."

"Don't worry about it."

"You'll be wanting to accept Harvey's job offer," he told her. "I think he means it, by the way."

"I'm sure he does," she said, looking amused. "But it's the last job I'd ever want. He'd be impossible to work for, far too nervous."

"Nervous?" Alan said in surprise. "That's not an adjective I'd apply to him. He's like an iceberg."

"I bet that's a front," Judith told him. "And I'm sure his wife and his secretary would both tell you he's a nervous wreck."

"Could be," Alan said, but he sounded doubtful. "I think I should pass along some of Harvey's gems of wisdom to the Mayor. Get him on the line for me."

Judith did this and then worked at her desk as Alan gave the Mayor a summary of the conversation between himself and Fred Harvey. The phone talk ended with Alan inviting the Mayor to his office later in the afternoon. When the young man hung up he called out to her, "The Mayor will be dropping by about four o'clock."

"Fine," Judith said. "I'll keep you clear of any appointments at that time."

"What have I for the rest of the day?" he wanted to know.

She rose from her desk and went in to stand by him. Checking the appointment book, she said, "The union representative at one-thirty. A Mrs. Regan about a property being sold to the bridge authority at two o'clock. After that there is only Mr. Stevens coming in to discuss his suit against the bus company."

Alan listened. "Doesn't sound too bad," he said. "It will give me time to work out some ideas for the Mayor." Then suddenly he groaned and clapped a hand to his temple. "I forgot Pauline!"

"You said she was in New York."

Alan shook his head. "She's getting back on this morning's plane. I told her to meet me here and we'd have lunch together."

"You can still manage that if you don't waste any time."

"It will make it tight," he mourned. "And I could have used that time to consider my plans. Now I'll have to spend the entire noon hour hearing Pauline talk about the marvelous paintings she picked up while she was away!"

Judith smiled. "Isn't she entitled to some enthusiasm for her work?"

He sighed. "All right; take her side. I guess I'll have to suffer through it. But when we leave, be sure to mention I have an appointment and have to be back early."

"Then she'll think I'm a cat with designs on you."

"Better that than that I overstay my lunch

hour with her," he said. And then his thin face brightened. "Maybe she won't come! Perhaps she'll decide to stay in New York another day."

But Pauline Walsh put in an appearance at exactly ten minutes to twelve. She was a tall, slim, blonde girl with a great deal of dash. She was wearing her hair in a short, graceful coiffure, and the suit she had on was of some satiny silver material. She wore tall boots of a matching shade, and her skirt line was enough above her knees to reveal a fetching pair of legs. Yet for her height she carried the short skirt very well.

She always politely referred to Judith as Miss Barnes, and as she swept into the outer office with a smile on her lovely face, she said, "Is Alan in, Miss Barnes?"

Judith got up. "Yes. He's expecting you."

"Grand!" Pauline rolled her eyes. "I was afraid with all his business problems, he'd forget about me."

"No chance of that." Judith smiled. "He's on the phone. As soon as he hangs up, I'll let him know you're here."

"I had a wonderful trip," Pauline went on in her breathless way. "Picked up some divine clothes for myself! Saw a lot of my old friends and discovered a great new talent for the gallery!"

"You must have been busy!"

"I didn't have an idle moment from the time I stepped off the plane," Pauline assured her. "I had the paintings sent on ahead. And I'm having a party to introduce them at the gallery on Friday night. Why don't you come?"

The abrupt invitation left Judith at a loss. "I'm afraid I'm not a good potential buyer," she confessed. "I haven't any spare money these days."

"That doesn't matter, darling!" Pauline protested in her breezy manner. "You have plenty of friends to tell about the paintings. You have good taste. You're exactly the type of person I want there."

"I'll think about it," Judith promised. "And thanks."

"You haven't been out much socially lately," Pauline said, studying her. "I'm sure you've been missed. It would do you good to come."

"I'd enjoy it, and I will try to be there."

"Be there!" Pauline insisted. And with a conspiratorial smile: "I'll tell Alan to make sure you don't offer any last minute excuses."

"He's off the line now," Judith said, grateful for a diversion. "I'll tell him you're here." And with this she ushered the blonde girl into Alan's office.

Not long afterward Pauline and Alan came out together on their way to lunch. Alan paused to give Judith a knowing glance and ask, "Just what do I have after I come back?"

"The appointment with the union representative at one-thirty," Judith said, taking her cue. "It's very important you be back in time for it."

Alan was as solemn as if the little dialogue hadn't all been pre-arranged. "I'll keep that in mind," he assured her.

As they went out the door, Pauline called back to her, "And don't you forget about Friday night!"

CHAPTER FIVE

Left to her own resources for the lunch hour, Judith decided that rather than hurry out somewhere for a quick snack, she would have a sandwich and milk sent in. This would leave her with some time to finish a novel she'd been enjoying in her rare free moments. Also, it would allow her to remain in the office and take any phone calls. There could be some important messages with the present crisis pending.

This decided, she phoned her order to the fountain service around the corner and settled down with her book. No phone calls came in and there were no interruptions by callers until the boy came with her lunch. After he had gone and she'd finished it, she checked the time. It was still a few minutes short of one o'clock, so Alan would not be back from his luncheon engagement for a half-hour. Again she relaxed to enjoy the novel.

She hadn't read more than a few lines when the office door opened and she raised her eyes to see Brandon Fraser come in.

"Is Alan back from lunch yet?" he asked.

78

She smiled. "No. Miss Walsh returned from New York, and they're having lunch together. I don't expect him until one-thirty."

"Oh!" The news didn't exactly seem to cheer the reserved head of the law firm. "Is he usually away from the office that long for lunch?"

"No," Judith said hastily. "He often has something sent in."

"I see." Brandon Fraser nodded, his lips tight again, as if he suspected she was trying to put a good front up for Alan and wasn't impressed by her assurance that Alan often had lunch as he worked.

To make it seem more convincing, she decided to add lamely, "Of course we have no set rule about it."

The gray-haired man's smile was cold. "So I gather," he said. His hands were clasped behind his back, and he stood ramrod straight, his deep-set eyes studying her. "How do you like working as my son's secretary?" he asked.

Judith managed a smile. "I'm very happy here," she said. "Of course I've known Mr. Fraser since school days."

"I'm aware of that," the precise voice said. "I haven't forgotten our families have been neighbors all these years. I know you call Alan by his first name. You needn't do otherwise for my benefit." He glanced around the office appraisingly. "I'm not a client to be impressed."

"No, sir," she said in a small voice.

Brandon Fraser continued his study of the office. "This place is shamefully shabby. I must see that it is redecorated in the same style as my own office." He gave her a sharp glance again. "It was too bad about your father," he said. "How is your mother these days?"

"She isn't too well," Judith said. "So she doesn't go out much."

"The last of the Melrose line," Brandon Fraser commented thoughtfully, "excluding yourself, of course. And I think of you as a Barnes. I'm afraid the Melrose blood ran a bit thin."

Judith was uneasy in the stern presence of the elder Fraser. "I have some cousins in Vermont," she ventured. "They're the closest relatives I have left."

The deep-set eyes fixed on her. "You used to go out with Alan, didn't you?"

"Long ago, during high school days," she said with a smile.

He stared at her in silence for a moment. "Yes, I remember. He brought you to the house quite a few times."

"Before he left for college," she said.

Brandon Fraser frowned. "I seem to remember seeing you even after that," he said. "Didn't you know my late son, Brian, as well?"

"Yes," she said quietly. "Brian and I went out together some."

The deep-set eyes glowed with pleasure. "Brian was a fine boy, wasn't he?"

"He was."

Alan's father was so deep in his own reverie that it was doubtful if he heard her. With a nod of his head, and almost as if he were talking solely for his own benefit, he said, "If Brian had lived, he would have had a brilliant future! First in sports, studies and everything! He put Alan to shame! If Brian had lived, he would be doing important work for the firm by now!"

Judith couldn't help saying, "How lucky that you still have Alan."

He stared at her with a blank expression on his granite face. Then he moved across the office to look out of the window into the alley, his back to her.

"Were you in love with my boy Brian?" he asked. "Would you have married him if he hadn't been killed?"

Judith was startled by the abruptness of the question. She hesitated as she sought for a proper way to reply.

With an effort, she said, "I liked Brian a good deal. But we weren't serious about each other."

Brandon Fraser kept his back to her. "I often wonder whom he would have married?"

Very quietly, she said, "I suppose that is only natural. I often try to imagine what would have happened had my father not died so suddenly."

"I would have had fine, sturdy grandchildren by now," Brandon Fraser said in his remote voice.

Judith felt a sense of guilt, as if she had allowed herself to be a party to the older man's unhealthier brooding about this older son whom he had plainly worshipped to the point of obsession.

She spoke up, saying, "Alan is doing important work now. You must be very proud of him. It was an honor, his being made chairman of the bridge authority."

Now the gray-haired man turned to her. "You think that?" he asked.

"Yes, of course."

"I'd like to believe it was an honor," Brandon Fraser said slowly. "But I am not by any means as sure as you appear to be."

"I don't understand," she faltered.

He brushed the matter aside with a swift gesture. "It's not important," he said. "I understand the Mayor is coming by here later this afternoon?"

"Yes," she said, hiding her surprise that he already was informed of this and wondering how much more he might know.

"Ask him to stop by my office a moment when he leaves," Alan's father said. "I'd like to speak to him."

"I will," she promised.

The gray-haired man hesitated. "Remember me to your mother."

Judith smiled. "She'll appreciate your thinking of her."

He nodded absently. "You and I must have a talk sometime."

Again she was surprised. "I'd enjoy that."

"I'd like to hear more of your impressions of Brian," he said. "It is almost like having him alive again to hear about him from someone who was a friend."

"Yes, of course," Judith said in a low voice, thoroughly embarrassed.

"You won't forget my message to the Mayor?" Brandon Fraser asked, his hand on the doorknob.

"No, Mr. Fraser," she said. "I'll be sure to mention that you wish to see him."

"Thank you," he said quietly, and went out.

Alan arrived back a few minutes before one-thirty, looking less than refreshed by his luncheon date with Pauline. He gave Judith a weary smile. "It was just as I told you. The whole noon hour I listened to the merits of this new artist she's featuring at the gallery."

Judith laughed. "At least it was a change."

"Not the kind I needed. The union man hasn't gotten here yet?"

"No. Your father came by a moment. He seemed to know the Mayor was coming in this afternoon and asked that he stop by his office on the way out."

Alan's eyebrows rose as he lingered by her desk. "Someone must have leaked the news. There are not many secrets kept at City Hall." Changing the subject, he added, "By the way, Pauline was very serious in inviting you to that party Friday. She wants you to come."

"I doubt that I'll be able to make it."

"You can if you want to," he told her. "And I think you should. I have an idea quite a few people we want information on will be there. It could be a great chance for you to mingle with them and find out what is on their minds."

"Now I'm to play the role of lady spy,"

she suggested archly.

Alan's face was bleak. "We may have need of one."

He went on inside, and almost as soon as he was seated at his desk the union representative arrived. He was a small, nondescript sort of man who acted as agent for the local. His name was Jack Smith, and he was as ordinary in every way as his name. She ushered him into Alan's office and at his signal left the door open so she was able to hear what was being said.

After the routine preliminary remarks, Alan got down to business. "Just what is on your mind?" he asked the union agent.

"We aren't happy with the working arrangements here," Smith said in a nasal twang. "We've got men working overtime and only being paid the regular hourly rate."

"I'm trying to keep to a tight budget," Alan pointed out. "And we pay those same men for doing nothing days when it's too stormy to work."

"I don't know about that," the union man said uneasily.

"It's true, just the same," was Alan's sharp reply.

"Also, we don't think the working conditions at the bridge are safe enough," the man went on. "The men are running too many risks."

"We're taking safety measures every day," Alan insisted. "If they have any suggestions for making conditions better, they should pass them on to us and not bellyache to the union about it; give us a chance to benefit by their suggestions."

"The feeling seems to be you wouldn't want to do that."

"I think I know our point of view on this better than you do," Alan said in a biting tone, "or your informants. We are anxious to work with the men."

"The union thinks they should have a new contract," the man went on doggedly. "An official will be coming in to hold talks and meetings. If we don't get the satisfaction we want, there'll be a strike."

Judith heard Alan jump up. "Are you threatening me with a strike?" he demanded angrily.

"I'm telling you facts," the union man whined. "We'll have our official here in a few days, ready to see you."

"And I'll be ready to see him!" Alan vowed.

The union man mumbled an unhappy goodbye and quickly made his way out. Alan came back to Judith's office to stand glaring at the door the union man had just closed after him.

He turned to her. "Well, at least trouble never comes in single lots."

"I had no idea the union business was so serious," she said.

Alan was angry. "It's not the men who want a strike; it's fellows like this one who live off the unions. They'll bring in an out-of-town organizer and try to stir up enough trouble to close us."

"Have they a chance of doing so?"

"I don't know," he said. "Maybe the Senator will manage to put them out of work first." He headed toward his office and as he prepared to close the door, he said, "Anyway, it looks as if we'll have to bargain with some out-of-town official."

Judith said, "I'll let you know when Mrs. Regan arrives."

The next two hours were busy ones, and by the time the Mayor showed up an exhausted Alan was out in Judith's office, joining her in a fast cup of hot coffee. Alan greeted the Mayor with the steaming paper cup in his hand.

With a forced smile, he said, "A bearer of glad tidings."

Mayor Jim Devlin stood there smiling at them both. "I only wish that was so," he said in his pleasant announcer's voice. He was a man of medium size and middle age. He had a square, strong face with a shrewd cast, relieved by generous blue eyes.

Alan asked, "Any further word from the Senator?"

"Lafferty has been on the line a half-dozen times today," Jim Devlin said, sinking into a handy chair wearily and giving the young lawyer a sharp glance. "Looks as if S.C. North is really out to buck the bridge!"

"But I thought that was all over!" Alan protested.

The Mayor nodded grimly. "I suppose that's what they wanted us to think. But apparently they've been biding their time. Now they're going to strike and strike hard."

"So Fred Harvey said this morning," Alan told him with a sigh. "You want Judith to pour you a cup of coffee?"

"I'd enjoy one," Jim Devlin said, offering her a smile. "Anyway, you've got a good-looking secretary, Alan, and that's one up on me."

Judith poured him the coffee he'd requested and passed the cup to him. "If Senator Lafferty keeps you as busy as he has today, you won't have time to notice pretty girls," she warned him.

The Mayor took a sip of his coffee. "You're not joking," he said. "I can't imagine why I left working behind a microphone for this job. And I can tell you I don't want any more of it."

"The rumor is you're not running again," Alan said.

Jim Devlin smiled. "I'm running in the opposite direction — right back to the television station and my sports show. I've had enough and plenty! It's the last quarter, and the game looks bad for the home team!"

Judith laughed. "You sound as if you were describing a game," she said.

"Boy oh boy!" The Mayor took another gulp of his coffee. "Who ever said politics was a place for an honest man?"

Alan smiled. "I think you did, in your campaign speeches."

"That shows the kind of an innocent I was then," Jim Devlin said, staring bleakly at his half-empty coffee cup. "Well, I know better now. With Fred Harvey away, that leaves eleven men on the council. Seven of them are owned by S.C. North in one way or another, and one of them is being groomed by him as the next Mayor. So no matter what I try to do, the majority is going to vote in favor of Senator Lafferty and his group on that petition."

"It's that bad?" Alan said.

"It's that bad." The Mayor sighed.

"So then what happens?" the young lawyer asked.

"They'll want to put the whole thing in the Governor's lap," the Mayor predicted. "Lafferty is on the right side of him and probably has some deal arranged. North will do the Governor the favor of backing him in the next election, and the Governor will see the bridge is delayed long enough to turn the steel contract over to the North company."

"Not while I'm chairman of the bridge authority," Alan said firmly.

The Mayor gave him a sad smile. "They'll expect you to resign. If you don't, North will have his trained seals at the paper write some editorials to force you out."

"And if I refuse to give up?" Alan asked.

The Mayor looked at him in wide-eyed surprise. "Now, Son, don't tell me you're still ignorant of the rules of this game. When S.C. North calls a play, you make it one way or another. If you don't, you'll wish you had never been a member of the team!"

Alan frowned. "It can't be that bad."

"It's so bad I want to be a common man again," Jim Devlin said earnestly. "I can do without this high office. My neck is on the chopping block every day, with some of North's crowd debating whether they'll drop the axe or not. I want to get away from it fast!"

Judith said, "Are you telling us that Alan won't be allowed to stay on as chairman once this thing gets rolling?"

"That is my assumption," the Mayor said unhappily. "The game is well under way, and that is how I read the score. Alan will be removed from the line-up and a substitute will take over the play."

"But that's wickedly unfair," Judith protested, "after all he's done to make the bridge possible, all the effort he's put into it."

"No one could agree with you more heartily than I," Jim Devlin said, his honest face grim. "And as long as I'm Mayor, I'll fight every last inch of the way with you. But that doesn't mean I'll be able to turn the tide. Senator Lafferty and the North team have been waiting for this moment to rouse to action, leap into the game, and wind up with a rousing victory!"

Alan smiled ruefully. "We could hope the Senator might take off on another of his alcoholic binges. They usually put him out of business for a week or so."

"I understand he has been having ulcer

trouble," the Mayor said gloomily, "so I think that fortuitous circumstance is highly unlikely."

"At least he'll have to come into the open with whatever he's going to fight us with tonight," Alan said. "After the council meeting we'll know exactly what he has in mind."

"I would assume so," Mayor Devlin said. "As chairman of the bridge authority, you'll have to be there."

"I don't want to get into any shouting match with the Senator," Alan said with a frown. "And that's the way he usually tries to put his points over."

"He's sly," the Mayor warned. "And although that North End Real Estate Owners Association is strictly a second scrub team, he'll make the best possible showing with it."

"Have the rest of the bridge authority members been notified?" Judith asked.

"I told my secretary to phone them about the meeting this morning," the Mayor said. "Maybe you better have Judith call them again."

"It's late," Alan said. "But a late notice is better than none, just in case your girl messed up." He shook his head. "And what a committee we have! A retired printer, an over-age housewife, one of S.C. North's legal staff, and a cousin of his wife who is a retired customs officer. They must have been picked for their gullibility!"

"Well, it was always understood that, aside from your own office, the bridge authority was just a token group to represent the public," the Mayor pointed out. "The ideas was that as long as we had a strong chairman in you and the council took an active interest, we'd be able to handle any problems."

"It hasn't worked out so well," Alan reminded him.

"Maybe that was what was intended," the Mayor said unhappily. "Since I've taken office, I've been the victim of so many double plays I don't know what's going on half the time."

Alan turned to Judith. "Better get those calls started. Useless or not, they've a right to be properly notified."

The Mayor stood up with a broad smile and patted Alan on the back. "That's the spirit, my boy. Let's show the North crowd we're not going to be kayoed in the first round!"

CHAPTER SIX

When Judith returned home that evening, she found her mother busy in the kitchen.

"I have some of my veal cutlets in tomato sauce that you like so well," she announced brightly from her post by the electric stove.

"They are always good," Judith encouraged her from the doorway. And the truth was that this particular dish was one of the better ones her mother prepared.

"Dinner is ready," Millicent said brightly. "I have hot biscuits to begin with and tomato juice. So don't wait until everything is spoiled."

Judith promised that she wouldn't and hurried up to wash. It had been a long, wearying day, and she was feeling exhausted and not very hungry. But knowing that her mother had probably been working hard all afternoon to get the meal ready, she made up her mind to show some enthusiasm even if it was spurious.

When she seated herself at the table, her mother at once began to question her. "I've been hearing about some special petition Senator Lafferty is presenting. It's been on television all day. He's heading a delegation calling on the city council this evening. It has something to do with the bridge, hasn't it?"

Judith purposely busied herself buttering a biscuit. "These look just too good."

"It has something to do with the bridge, hasn't it?" her mother repeated in a querulous voice.

Judith glanced across the table with an expression of resignation. "I really can't tell you much about it yet, Mother," she said. "Senator Lafferty is trying to cause some trouble and delay the bridge."

Millicent's pale face under the lifeless, frizzled brown hair showed annoyance. "But you must know all the details! You're Alan Fraser's secretary, and he's chairman of the bridge authority."

Judith sipped her juice and tried to control her own rising anger. If only her mother would give her a few minutes to enjoy the meal! She said, "We don't know much more than you."

Millicent tossed her head. "Of course if you feel you can't trust your own mother, I suppose you have a right to keep quiet."

"It's not that!"

"I can't imagine why else you'd refuse to tell me anything," Millicent said tartly.

"Just like your father. He wouldn't ever discuss his business with me, and look where it landed him!"

"Please don't drag Father into this," Judith pleaded. "Whenever you want to hurt me, you bring up his name."

"Touchy! But you don't mind hurting my feelings with your silence."

"I'm not trying to hurt your feelings," Judith protested. "Anything I'd tell you now would be nothing more than guesses. And they mightn't be right at that. When I'm sure of my facts, I'll be glad to tell you what I know."

"I'm used to being treated like a child," her mother said with exaggerated resignation, "first by your father and now by you."

Judith said, "Brandon Fraser was inquiring about you today."

The prematurely withered face took on a pleased smile. "Was he really?"

"Yes. We had quite a long chat at noon. And he seemed in quite a nostalgic mood."

"And what did he say about me?" Millicent asked eagerly.

Judith held back a smile. "He inquired about your health and said he missed seeing you, that you should go out more often."

Millicent sighed. "I wouldn't want him to take a close look at me now. I've faded to nothing since all the trouble and your father's death."

"I wasn't going to say anything like that to him. I told him you hadn't been feeling yourself, but you hoped to get around again this summer."

Her mother sighed pensively. "I only wish that was true."

"You could at least work in the back garden," Judith suggested. "It would give you some air and sunshine. You needn't do much. And when neighbors came by, you'd have a chance to chat with them informally, pick up some old threads of friendship."

Her mother assumed an attitude of dejection, lingering over her plate. "I haven't wanted to. You know that. I feel they are all staring at me, whispering about me, talking about your father's bankruptcy, wondering how we are making ends meet!"

"That's all in your mind," Judith said firmly. "I have to meet the public, and so should you."

"You're different!" her mother protested. "You're not at all sensitive. You take after your father's people."

Judith bent over her plate to conceal her annoyance. "I still say Brandon Fraser showed interest in you, and you should be pleased."

"I am."

"He also brought up the fact that we had lived close to each other for a number of years."

"That is true," her mother said happily. "The Melroses and the Frasers were good friends ages ago, long before your father and I came to live here."

"He doesn't seem too happy a man," Judith went on. "He keeps mourning for Brian. I should think that would be over by now."

Her mother frowned. "Brandon Fraser is not that type, my dear. We members of fine old families take the loss of an elder son as a devastating blow. It is quite understandable that he should grieve."

"But he is so lucky to have a son like Alan!"

"I have no doubt Alan is a fine boy," her mother agreed. "But still, he does not take the place in his father's heart and hopes of poor Brian."

"So it seems," Judith said disconsolately.

"It seems to me," her mother said with a certain coyness, "that Brandon Fraser must be showing quite an interest in you."

"Not really. He just happened to come into the office."

Her mother's eyes were bright and knowing. "But he did talk to you about family. And I'm sure he's wondering the same thing as I am: why you and Alan don't realize how right you are for each other!"

Judith groaned. "Oh, Mother, don't start that again."

"I mean it for your own good," Millicent replied. "After what I saw last night, I know it's purely your fault if he doesn't ask you to marry him!"

Judith couldn't restrain a small burst of hopeless laughter. "Mother, you're positively mid-Victorian! You peek out through the curtains when you have no right to and see a man kissing me, and at once you think we should be married."

"It showed he's fond of you!" Millicent said stubbornly.

"All right, so we like each other!" Judith admitted. "And he kissed me good night on the doorstep. You surely don't think it was anything more than a polite gesture, like shaking hands or wishing me luck!"

"It meant a good deal more in my day," her mother said primly.

"Honestly," Judith said in despair, "I sometimes think you stepped right out of the pages of Godey's Lady's Book into the twentieth century. What do you think a kiss means today?"

Millicent got up indignantly and gathered the dirty plates. "I have no doubt my ideas are old-fashioned and out of date. But I would much rather live by my standards than by those of your generation, which engages in all kinds of degrading acts in the back seats of cars in drive-in theatres!" She retreated to the kitchen in a rage.

"I haven't been to a drive-in more than a half-dozen times in my life," Judith said angrily. "And at least a couple of times I went with girl friends. It happens I don't care for drive-ins. And anyway, they're not nearly as bad as you say they are. I don't suppose young people of your generation ever parked on side roads in model A Fords or some other kind of cars! You're being unfair!"

Millicent responded by giving her the silent treatment. It was her favorite means of showing Judith she couldn't be reasoned with. Judith silently accepted her dessert and went along with her mother's new mood. It was the simplest way.

It was over coffee that Millicent finally chose to find her voice and say, "I should think you'd be needed at that meeting tonight."

Judith said, "I'm not needed, but I do feel

I should be there to hear what goes on."

"Then why don't you go?"

Judith was surprised at her mother's reaction. Usually Millicent was anxious to have her stay home. With a questioning glance, she said, "Do you think I ought to?"

"Yes, I do," Millicent said definitely. "And I'm sure Alan Fraser would appreciate it as well."

Judith gave her mother a reproving smile. "You're not trying to match-make again?"

"Of course not," her mother said in a prim voice. "I'm more concerned about your job."

Judith sat back with a sigh. "It's at times like this I wish we still had a car," she said. "If I hurry, I guess I can catch the quarter-to-eight bus."

"Surely you can afford a taxi for an occasion like this," her mother said. "Then you won't have to rush so."

Judith laughed. "You're right! I'm so used to pinching pennies I've eliminated taxis from my world. But tonight shall be an exception."

"Take one home as well," her mother said, "unless someone you know offers you a drive back. I don't want you walking up the dark hill from the bus stop alone."

Judith got up, went over and kissed her

mother affectionately on the forehead. "Very well, Mother. And mind you don't worry!"

Millicent called after her as she started upstairs, "I'll certainly expect a little more information from you than you were able to give me earlier tonight when you get back."

When Judith got out of the taxi in front of the courthouse, she saw there were a large number of cars parked there. Without a doubt the council meeting had attracted a large crowd. Since it was close to eight, it was almost time for it to begin.

She hurried up the winding stairway to the top floor of the old building where the council meetings were held. As she neared the top, she was able to hear a murmur of voices from the crowded room. She edged her way in and saw that the spectators' benches were crowded. A friendly-faced young man in working clothes smiled at her and rose to give her his seat at the end of the bench nearest the door. Judith nodded her thanks and sat down.

The faces near her were mostly male and all strangers. There were a few older women scattered through the crowd, and she supposed these would be members of the real estate association. As she cast her eyes further afield in her survey of the room, she saw a serious-faced Alan seated to the right and near the front.

Then the council meeting began, and her attention was riveted to the happenings in the front of the big room. Mayor Jim Devlin conducted the meeting with an authority she found revealing in the normally easygoing man. There were a number of routine items before the matter that concerned her most was brought up.

She saw Senator Lafferty rise, a solemn expression on his pouting, bloated face as he began to read from his petition in his resonant courtroom voice. The Mayor stared gloomily at his desk top during the performance, and not until the Senator had finished and placed the petition on his desk did Devlin turn to the members of the council seated in a semicircle around him and say, "You have heard this petition. What is your pleasure, gentlemen?"

A sour-faced councilman with thick glasses was the first to speak up in a nasal twang. He asked, "Am I to understand the Senator claims bad faith toward the North End of the city in the way the bridge plans have been developed? And is he asking us to delay further construction until the matter is threshed over again?"

"That is essentially it," Mayor Devlin conceded.

The sour-faced councilman threw up his hands indignantly. "Worst kind of nonsense I've ever heard. If he wants to wreck the bridge, why doesn't he toss a bomb at it and get it over with!"

This brought laughter, boos and general confusion. In the melee of voices no one could be heard, and Mayor Devlin banged his gavel a number of times for silence.

Senator Lafferty was quickly on his feet, a supercilious smile on his florid alcoholic's face. "The councilman is making the issue too simple," he said in his easy way. "The minutes of earlier council meetings will show that a spur to the North End was considered and the public was not properly notified when the design of the bridge was decided on without that vital ingress to this important section of our fair city. This room is filled with taxpayers who will suffer if the completion of the bridge is rushed through and their welfare not considered."

There was a roar of approval and clapping from the section of the taxpayers' association gathered near the front of the room, and the Senator bowed his appreciation and sat down, smiling.

Mayor Devlin cleared his throat. "I believe the public was properly notified of the approved design of the bridge," he said. "The chairman of the bridge authority is in the room. Would he please stand and clarify this point?"

Alan quickly rose, and there was a murmuring from the taxpayers' group. He hesitated a moment for silence and then, addressing the mayor, said, "News items clearly indicated the final design of the bridge. We showed models of it in several locations, including one of the large department stories. There were programs concerning it on both radio and television. I feel we did all we could to let the citizens know what was happening."

As he sat down, various members of the council took up the debate. It became a heated one, and it was all the Mayor could do to keep reasonable order. As the different councilmen offered their opinions, it was easy for Judith to pick out those favoring the S.C. North interests. They lost no time in agreeing with the Senator that he was presenting a just complaint.

Senator Lafferty sprang to his feet again and in his most unctuous tone said, "I believe it would be possible for us to argue the various points for days and reach no agreement. I submit that an outside authority should look into this complaint and make an objective decision. Therefore, let us turn it over to the state and have a Governor's committee say whether or not the basic design of the bridge should be changed to include a North End spur."

There were cheers and loud applause and a stamping that made the old building tremble. Judith felt she could shed tears of frustration and, glancing at Alan, saw that he'd gone quite pale. It wasn't hard to judge the tenor of the meeting. The Senator had played his wily game for S.C. North well, and it seemed that everything the absent Fred Harvey and the Mayor had predicted was going to happen.

Mayor Devlin pounded his gavel for order. "I guess we have reached the point where this calls for a vote," he said in a grim voice.

Judith watched tensely as the vote was taken. It was seven to four in favor of turning the problem over to the state. It seemed that S.C. North and his front, as represented by Senator Lafferty and the North End Real Estate Owners Association, had won this round. The meeting was declared adjourned, and Judith rose, to be jostled by the surging crowd as she headed toward the stairs in a depressed state of mind.

The crowd was an unruly one, and she

found herself pushed forward toward the stairs in a frightening way. It was as if she were being propelled ahead by an angry wave. The stairs were steep, and she became afraid that she might stumble and be trampled on by the heedless group surging around her.

Then she felt someone take her arm and glanced up to see that it was Alan. She felt relief at having him to depend on. He gave her an inquiring glance.

"You didn't tell me you planned to come here," he said.

She managed a wan smile. "I didn't make up my mind until the last minute."

Alan struggled to keep them from being shoved about by the impatient crowd, bent only on getting down the stairs in the least possible time. "Stay close to me," he told her, "and I'll see if we can get out of here without being torn to bits."

The next few minutes were given over entirely to a descent of the steep, winding stairs. When they emerged in the refreshing cool air of the early summer evening at last, she gave a deep sigh of thankfulness.

"That was some experience!" she exclaimed, glancing toward the doors of the courthouse from which the noisy crowd was still spewing.

Alan nodded grimly. "One I could easily do without," he said. "what did you make of it all?"

"Senator Lafferty played the comedy out like a veteran," she replied. "I'm sure it was all cut and dried. He knew exactly how the vote was going to go."

"So it seems," Alan said. They were standing on the edge of the sidewalk a little distance from the entrance to the courthouse.

"What happens now?"

"A report of the vote will be turned over to me as chairman of the bridge authority. Then the petition will go to Concord for the Governor to consider and act upon it."

"And after that?"

"I'll undoubtedly receive instructions to halt work on the bridge until the matter is settled," he said. "If a North End spur is to be added, it will have to be done before we begin the second half of the structure."

"I see," she said bleakly. "Then the work will go on for a few days, anyway."

"Possibly a few weeks," Alan said. "It will depend on the Governor's agenda. If he's busy, he may take some time getting around to it. But sooner or later it means calling a halt." He paused. "My car is down the block. I'll drive you home."

When they were in the car and driving down King Street, he glanced at her and said, "I don't feel much like going home yet, and I'm not hungry, so a restaurant isn't in order. Do you mind if I just drive around for a while?"

She smiled in the shadows of the car's front seat. "Just as long as you don't take me to a drive-in."

He gave her a startled glance. "What's that?"

"Pay no attention to me," she said. "It's a private joke." And she huddled down comfortably against the seat. "Drive as long as you like. I don't feel like going directly home, either."

So Alan drove aimlessly through the night-cloaked streets in an effort to dispel the restless, troubled feelings that ran deep in both of them. Perhaps it was inevitable that he should finally park the big car on a hill beside an old church in the West End of the city that offered a fine view of the construction site. The completed spans of the bridge were marked with lights that gave the illusion it was already being finished and ready for traffic, except for the gaping black void where the steel had not been put in place at the eastern approach.

Alan stared at the distant lights. "Do you

think this is the beginning of the end?" he asked.

For his sake, Judith simulated a confidence she didn't really feel. "You've made a fine start, and I think it's too late for them to ruin things now."

"I'd like to believe that," he said pensively. "I'm afraid it's not so."

Judith studied him with troubled eyes. "I think it's especially important that you believe you can win out, that you have confidence in yourself."

He turned to her. "Of course you're right," he said. "But the truth is that I haven't much foundation for confidence. It seems to me that up to now I've done nothing but make a muddle of my life."

"You're not being fair to yourself," she protested.

"Let's look at things objectively," he said. "From the beginning, I've tried to please Father by emulating Brian. And it hasn't worked. He feels I'm inferior, and deep down, so do I. Instead of measuring myself against what I've been able to accomplish, I've insisted on following Father's example and comparing what I've managed to do with what Brian would have done if he'd lived."

"That's stupid!" Judith exclaimed. "I

knew Brian well enough to be certain he wasn't the confident golden boy your father pictures in his imagination. He was as insecure as any of us. There's no telling whether he would have accomplished even as much as you have. It's unfair to his memory and to your own abilities to go on trying to use Brian as a barometer of your achievements."

He smiled at her. "You sound very worked up on the subject."

"Because I know how important it is that you see clearly now!"

"Thanks, Judith," he said. "I can't forget that my most stupid mistake was giving you up because I thought Brian was interested in you. Following my usual practice, I turned my back on a situation I didn't understand."

"It doesn't matter now," she said softly.

Alan sighed. "At this point it all adds up to one gigantic failure!"

"Another exaggeration," she said. "But if you feel that up to now you've been wrong, make this the time for a new start."

He nodded. "I can try. And let me begin by telling you that if I'm sure about any one thing, it's that I'm in love with you!" And he took her in his arms.

CHAPTER SEVEN

Judith couldn't pretend Alan's embrace was unexpected, but the strong declaration of his love for her certainly was. And the ardent manner in which his lips caressed hers underlined what he had said in a way that left little room for dispute or doubt on her part. Although she was fully aware he was engaged to another girl, she felt a glowing happiness and a sense of rightness in feeling his arms around her.

At least he released her a little, his arms still about her, and stared down at her with a sober look on his sensitive face. "I can't pretend any longer," he said. "You're the only girl who has ever counted in my life."

"Alan!" she said gently in utter confusion. And then, "What about Pauline?"

"Pauline is a wonderful person and a good friend," he said wearily. "I've played her a mean trick. I let us become engaged, knowing I didn't love her."

"You must have felt something!"

"Loneliness and despair at losing you," he said. "Pauline was merely a substitute for the person I'd given up hoping to have — you!"

She shook her head. "I don't know, Alan!"

"Make up your mind," he said quietly. "One minute you're telling me to take stock and build myself a new life. When I attempt to begin by admitting the truth about my feelings, you beg me to be a hypocrite."

"No!"

"Either I begin honestly or I don't," he said.

"I'm thinking about Pauline."

"She'll understand," he assured her. "It's better to be frank to her about my feelings than to allow her to make a second fraudulent marriage."

Judith knew there was strong truth in his words, but she still hesitated.

"Alan," she said in a low troubled voice, "however much I want to help you, there is still my side of it. It seems to me you're forgetting about my feelings in this. All I've heard is your great need for my love. You haven't discussed how I feel about you!"

He frowned. "Are you saying you don't love me?"

"No," she said. "I'm trying to make you understand that in the years we've been apart, I've had to make my own adjustments as well. You're bringing all this to a head so suddenly that you're leaving me uncertain. I'm not sure that I'm still in love with you."

"I don't understand."

She sighed. "Give us a little time, Alan. Let me think about it and get used to the idea. And you consider as well. It could be that in the end you'll discover it's Pauline who would make the best wife for you after all." Alan was silent a moment. "Are you trying to say you think you may still be in love with Miles Estey?"

"Why do you ask that?"

"Because that's what I think this indecision on your part means."

"I don't agree."

"Can you honestly tell me you no longer have any love for Miles?"

"We were going to be married," she reminded him.

"I know that. You haven't answered my question."

She smiled wanly. "Before, you said you were in love with me. Yesterday, I might have been willing to admit that it was all over with Miles; that he had been merely a substitute for you, as you say Pauline was for me. But now that I am faced with a final decision, I can't be that sure. Perhaps I'd have to see Miles again and talk with him before I could really know."

"I see," he said unhappily. "In other words, my indecision may have caused me to lose you."

"Not necessarily," she said. "Let us take this in our stride calmly, give ourselves time to be truly certain. That's the only way we can be fair to each other and to Pauline and Miles."

"Meanwhile, you know where I stand."

She nodded, her eyes bright with happiness. "I know," she said softly. "And I want you to realize how much you mean to me and be strong, no matter what problems arise in the days ahead."

"I have to be satisfied with that?"

"It's all I can offer now," she said.

He sighed. "Then it will have to do." And he pressed her close to him for another long kiss.

On the drive back to Mount Pleasant, he began to talk of other things, chiefly his problem with his father. "I'm not sure I should have gone into the firm with him now," he said. "When this present crisis is over, I think I'll either strike out on my own or join another firm."

"It might be better," she agreed. "You can see how things develop."

"Dad is friendly with North as well," Alan

went on, "although I can't say the firm gets much business from the North enterprises. Having their own legal firm, they don't need us. But my opposing the establishment this way is probably causing Dad some headaches."

"I can't see how he can criticize you for your stand," she said.

"Nor will he endorse it," Alan said. "And I shouldn't need his endorsement. Whatever I do about this, I should make it clear it's my own decision. The actions I take will be my own. I want the Senator and North to know that."

"At least you have one good friend," she said. "Fred Harvey."

"I wish he hadn't gone to Washington," Alan said, his attention on driving through the midnight streets. "I could use him here for advice at this time."

"He seemed to think you should chart this out on your own."

"I gathered that," he agreed with a slight frown. "I'm not sure I think he was right in suggesting I go along with the decision on the bridge, whatever it may be. I can't picture myself agreeing to stay on as chairman if the North End spur is authorized."

"Fred Harvey seemed very sure it would be."

"Which is a pretty fair guarantee that it will be."

"I'd expect him to be encouraging you to oppose North," she said. "Instead, he seemed to think you might gain more in the end by going along with him."

"Fred Harvey is sly," Alan reminded her. "Whatever he has in mind, it's first going to be for the benefit of Fred Harvey. Secondly, no matter what he may say, underneath he is North's most dangerous opponent. I can't begin to fathom what he has in mind concerning the bridge, but he must see some ultimate twist that will make it possible for him to turn the tables on North, the Senator and that whole gang."

She sighed. "It seems that S.C. North is bound to play a part in my life," she said.

"Since you live in Port Winter, that goes without saying."

"I mean in a personal way," she said. "It's not only that we are forced to do business with him through a dozen different firms and services, but he has actively opposed both the men in my life: first Miles Estey and now you."

Alan laughed shortly. "I hadn't thought of that before. It's true. You think Miles did actually get a bad deal here?"

"I know it," she said emphatically. "If

North had really sound proof that Miles embezzled money from the timber company, he would have had the authorities on him in no time. Instead, he allowed Miles to leave under a cloud. And I'm certain he did it to shift the blame from his own son. I've no doubt Charles North was responsible for the thefts."

"It sounds reasonable," Alan agreed. "But why didn't Miles fight the charges?"

"You shouldn't have to ask that," she said with some scorn. "You know better than most people the chances of winning a fight against S.C. North in this town. They probably had enough rigged evidence to convict Miles if he had been foolish enough to deny the theft."

"So he left knowing that he was innocent but unable to do anything about it."

"He couldn't stay here. There was nothing for him. And I believe North has seen to it that his reputation as a thief has followed him."

"You haven't heard from Miles lately?"

"No. He was very bitter. I can't imagine what's happened or where he's gone."

They were in front of her place now. Alan shut off the motor and turned to her. "I'll talk to Pauline about us as soon as I can," he promised.

"Don't be too hasty," she warned. "You'll have enough on your mind with the Senator pushing his bridge plans in the next few days."

"Are you trying to say you don't love me?"

"We've been over that ground thoroughly. No! Just try to be patient." She smiled at him. "And, Alan, if you're going to kiss me good night, please do it here in the car and not on the steps. My mother happens to have a peeping-Tom complex!"

"Anything to oblige a lady," he said easily, and drew her to him once more for a parting kiss.

Thus it was that a new understanding between them came about. But there was no surface hint of it when they met in the office the next morning. Alan was anxious to get all his routine business out of the way early in the day so he could then devote his energies to the crisis created by the Senator's petition.

They were making good headway when Alan's father put in an appearance. As soon as the thin, patrician Brandon Fraser stepped through the doorway, Judith was aware that he was in an ugly mood. His deep-set eyes gave her a passing glance as he offered her a faint nod of greeting and strode into his son's office. Judith bent over her typewriter, knowing she was going to be witness to an unpleasant interlude that she would have preferred to miss.

Alan spoke first in a pleasant tone. "We don't usually see you this early in the morning, Dad."

Brandon Fraser's words were biting. "I don't often open my morning paper to such a disappointing headline."

"You mean the bridge?"

"What else do you think I could mean?" The older man's attitude was one of accusation. "So you've managed to blunder this as well!"

"Just a minute, Dad," Alan said placatingly. "I can't see how you hope to place the blame on me. It's Senator Lafferty who is upsetting the apple cart. He's deliberately trying to throw chaos into our present plans so North's crowd can take over. S.C. wants the steel contract for the balance of the construction. He's never gotten over being turned down by my committee."

"Are you suggesting that a man of S.C. North's stature would be interested in battling with you?" Brandon Fraser demanded with incredulous disgust.

"The issue may not be exactly that simple," Alan said in a voice showing his growing anger. "But it does amount to that, I suppose. As the present chairman of the bridge authority, I've stood in his way. He intends to get rid of me."

"You flatter yourself in thinking you have that much importance!" Brandon Fraser snapped.

"I think I'm keeping things in perspective," Alan told him. "I refuse to join the local cult of S.C. North worshippers. I am fully aware he is a human being the same as the rest of us, with all the weaknesses which are universally shared."

"Your philosophy is more impressive than your record of success," his father said in his cold rage. "My only solace is that I had a son who, if he'd lived, would have done me proud; not wound up in a mess like this."

"Isn't that a fairly wild guess on your part, Dad?" Alan asked evenly.

"What are you saying?" Brandon Fraser sounded startled.

"I'm telling you that it's ridiculous of you to pretend to know what Brian would have done had he lived. It's time you realized that!"

"Are you trying to cast reflections on my dead son, your brother!"

"I'm asking you to stop deceiving yourself," Alan said quietly.

There was a long silence from the other room. Judith could picture the two men standing there facing each other.

"So that's your defense," Brandon Fraser said at last in a voice scarcely above a whisper. "You are trying to hide behind Brian in death as you did in life. You're a second-rater, and you always were one!"

Alan made no reply to his enraged parent. A moment later Brandon Fraser rushed out of the room and made straight for the corridor without glancing or looking back. The door slammed closed after his angry exit. Judith sat at her desk, stunned.

Alan came out to offer her a rueful smile. "Well, I made a start. I'm not sure that I managed it very tactfully."

"You defended yourself as you had a right to do," she told him, still indignant at the behavior of the elder Fraser.

Alan nodded. "He didn't know how to take it. It was a novel situation for him. I don't think I've ever given him a straight opinion before."

"It will do him good."

"He certainly reacted strongly," Alan said.

"Let him think it over," she suggested, "get used to the idea that you can stand on your own feet. Next time he may not be so ready to attack you."

The young lawyer's face was grave. "I hate to hurt him. That's why I've always refrained from mentioning Brian until now."

"It's past time," she assured him. "You have to hurt him to help him."

"Let's hope you're right," he said, doubt in his voice.

The balance of the morning was an anticlimax after this scene. Several clients showed up for appointments, and the Mayor called and promised he would drop by right after the lunch hour. Judith applied herself to her work and tried to get the unpleasant scene between father and son out of her mind.

She was also nagged by her doubts. It wasn't too hard to put up a brave front for Alan's benefit, but she couldn't deceive herself so easily. She had the conviction that things were going to be more difficult before they became better. And while Alan had made a good beginning, she was still not so sure that he wouldn't revert to type and, when things got really bad, simply turn his back on them and walk away.

She would have liked to have marched into Brandon Fraser's office and given him a lecture about his cruelty to his son. But she could see that this would be pointless.

The lunch hour was over and most of the routine work safely looked after when Mayor Jim Devlin entered the office with his usual jaunty smile.

Coming over to stand by Judith, he gave her one of his fond glances. "I spotted you out among the peasants last night," he said. "I had no idea I'd charmed you so you'd come to watch me preside over the council."

"I was swept away by your performance," she assured him.

"And almost down the courthouse stairs as well," Alan said, coming out of his office to join them. "If I hadn't come to her rescue when the meeting ended, they'd have trampled her underfoot."

"Unruly crowd!" the Mayor agreed. And with spread hands, he added, "Well, it worked out just about as we expected."

"As you expected," Alan corrected him.

"I thought Senator Lafferty was in fine fettle," the Mayor said. "North must have made the stakes for this job plenty high."

"When do I get my official notice from the council?" Alan wanted to know.

"My secretary is working on the copies now," the Mayor said. "Copies of the petition and the council minutes will be in the mail and should reach you the first of the week."

"So we've got a little time," Alan said.

"None to squander," the Mayor warned. "I hear the Governor is going to clear the slate to give this matter his urgent attention."

Alan frowned. "So whatever is done had better be done quickly."

The Mayor walked over and seated himself in a chair, his soft hat pushed to the back of his head, looking more like a sports commentator than the Mayor of a fairly large city.

"I'd say you'd have to streak down the field plenty fast to save this game," he said.

Alan smiled wanly. "You're the coach. Got any ideas?"

"I wish I had," Mayor Devlin said, his expression thoughtful. "I've read the petition over and gone into the background of it all. Beyond the fact they've waited past the proper time to make the complaint, you can't put your finger on anything wrong they've done."

"So it seems," Alan agreed.

"The Senator is slick," the Mayor went on. "He's made this a truly righteous cause."

"Of course we know that's not so," Judith

interrupted. "It's only that S.C. North wants to defeat Alan and get the steel contract."

Mayor Devlin's head was on one side, and he gave her one of his thoughtful smiles. "We know that, but we've got to think how this looks to the public. And I can tell you the Senator has rigged up a mighty righteous appeal. If only we could catch a hint of some ulterior motive."

"I think I follow you," Alan said.

"But it's so pure!" the Mayor went on. "Almost too pure!" He gave Alan a stern glance. "There must be something!"

"It could be the Senator's first honest venture," Judith said with a strong note of doubt.

"Preposterous!" the Mayor said, standing up. "It's a point of honor with him to be crooked." He began to pace slowly back and forth. "I'd say we have only one chance to defeat them; just one chance to show them up before the public for the charlatans they are. And that's to find out what private trickery the Senator has been up to in this deal."

"If there is any," Alan said.

"Has to be," the Mayor assured him. "I told you dishonesty is inherent in the man's nature. That's how he got in trouble with

S.C. North before. He tried to include some extra gravy for himself when he was doing some dirty work for the big man. North let him go and almost didn't take him back."

"You think he may be repeating himself this time?" Alan asked.

The Mayor paused to give him an encouraging glance. "I'm almost sure of it. But unless we can dig up something, we're not going to get far. And the Senator is running scared these days. He'll be bound to have his tracks covered cleverly."

Judith considered. "Just what could he gain on the side?"

Mayor Jim Devlin pursed his lips. "Well, let's think who would benefit most by the North End spur. Number one, there's the big shopping plaza. Now if the Senator should hold any shares in it, or be the recipient of a yearly retainer from them, it wouldn't look so good. We'd have a strong point of self-interest right there!"

Alan nodded quickly. "It shouldn't be too hard to find out if he's associated with the company which owns the plaza."

"I'd work on it," the Mayor told him. "And for a second try, see what you can find out about that big housing project they're building just on the other side of the shopping center. If the Senator has any connection with it, I'd say it would be just as good material to use against him."

Judith shook her head dubiously. "As you say, he's probably covered his tracks well."

"Dig deep!" the Mayor suggested. "What we need is something to show the Senator isn't riding into battle pure in heart and on a white charger. We want to smear him the same way he manages to smear anyone who opposes him or North. And I think if we work hard enough, it can be done."

"Knowing the Senator's feet are undoubtedly solid clay, it's worth a hard try," Alan agreed.

"Blow the whistle and let the game begin," the Mayor said with a grin. "You may bring home the silver trophy yet!"

"I think you have a sound idea," Alan said with fresh enthusiasm. "Instead of sitting around worrying about the dirty trick being played, we can gain more by using the same methods against them they are using on us."

"It seems I have inspired you to low and devious actions," Mayor Devlin said happily. "I can only promise you they have brought success to a host of people and wish you well."

"Come by when you have any other underhanded inspirations," Alan told him. "We have real need of them here."

The Mayor nodded and went to the door. Turning, he told them both, "Remember! Dig deep!"

When he'd gone, Judith turned to Alan with a smile. "What do you make of all that?"

"I think he's given us something to hope for."

"You put that much faith in his suggestions?"

Alan nodded. "It's all so basic we should have thought of it on our own. But then I guess we haven't political minds. The main fact is that we know Senator Lafferty is a natural crook. He's the weakest link in North's chain, even though North has to make use of him."

Judith began to feel a little of the young lawyer's excitement. "So the first thing to do is check and see if we can connect the Senator with the shopping center or the housing project."

"If we can do that, we're in," he said. "The Mayor is right. Our best way to win is by proving there's more behind the petition than a desire to protect the people of the North End." He smiled. "We may have to dig in the mud some ourselves, but I have the feeling it will be worth it."

"Where do you begin?"

"First, I'll find out who is representing the shopping plaza in the legal field. Then we'll dig to get a list of local stockholders."

CHAPTER EIGHT

Millicent Barnes was delighted at the news that Judith intended to go to Pauline Walsh's party. Her happy frame of mind was only slightly marred by what she had read about the petition to the city council concerning the bridge.

"I must say," she told Judith dolefully as she stood in her room watching her try on one of her cocktail dresses, "that the newspaper accounts don't put Alan Fraser in too happy a light."

"They aren't intended to," Judith said, studying the dress in her mirror. "Don't forget S.C. North owns the paper."

"Well, I don't see what that has to do with it!" her mother exclaimed.

"I thought I made it clear to you last night," Judith said, glancing at her. And then, seeing the perplexed look on her mother's pale face, she gave it up as useless. "Don't worry about it!"

"But I can't help worrying," Millicent said. "If Alan is as smart as you claim he is, how could he have made such a blunder?"

"I think I'll have to shorten this an inch or

so," Judith said, holding it up to judge.

"What I mean is," her mother went on, "he ought to have made sure the public knew what he was doing. I'm sure the North End people would have protested at once if they'd had any idea the spur to their part of the city had been dropped."

Judith sighed and quickly slipped the green dress up over her head. "I hope I have the right shade thread," she said. "I won't have more than time to do this if I'm going to wear it tonight."

"The editorials called it the error of a young and inexperienced man," Millicent said forlornly, sticking to the subject. "But they pointed out it had caused just as much trouble as if he'd done it deliberately."

"Ah!" Judith said with satisfaction as she bent over the sewing basket in which she kept her thread. "I do have almost a full spool. I'm in luck for once." And she took out a needle and the thread, prepared to hem the party dress.

Her mother meanwhile continued to fret about the newspaper stories. "I don't think the paper would print anything like that if they didn't think it was true. I'd say it looks as if he might lose his position as chairman."

Judith was seated with her dress and threading the needle. "Don't worry about it," she advised her mother.

"Well, it could mean your job as well. I can't help worrying."

"It will be all right," Judith promised, as she folded the hem and pinned it preparatory to tacking it up. "I don't know why skirts have to be worn so high!"

Millicent Barnes looked happier. "We have to follow the styles, dear. I don't know how many different skirt lengths I've seen fashionable in my time. And you should be glad you were invited to the party."

"I'm not sure I should go," Judith said as she began to sew.

"Why not?"

"I don't know whether I'll enjoy it. I've been away from that group so long I'm sure I can do without them."

"It's not healthy for you to stay in every night. You need some outside life."

"You should criticize!"

"Well, I'm older," Millicent said. "I've had my day."

"You talk like a great-grandmother, not a mother!" Judith protested.

"Well, it's true," her mother said with a sigh. And then, coyly, "Is Alan coming to take you?"

"As a matter of fact, he is," Judith said. "But don't go getting any ideas. He's engaged to Pauline, and she's the one giving the party. And he isn't taking her because she's already there getting things ready for later."

"I'm not getting any ideas," Millicent said angrily. "Surely a mother has a right to take an interest in her own little girl."

"I know the signs," Judith said calmly. "And it's been some time since I was a little girl."

"You will always be that to me," her mother said.

"Oh, Mother!" Judith groaned as she went on sewing.

"It isn't easy trying to be both a mother and father to you," Millicent said tartly. "I've done my best, but you seem to delight in going against me and making it harder."

"I'm sorry," Judith said, humoring her and privately thinking that she was the one who had to assume the responsibility in the household her mother should have taken.

Millicent had a happy thought. "Even though Alan Fraser is engaged, he could still change his mind. He may decide this other young woman is not right for him."

"That's true, Mother," Judith said, concentrating on her sewing, "Don't ever give up hope."

"You shouldn't make fun of such things!"

"I mean it."

Her mother sighed and started for the door. "Well, I hope you have a nice time. It's a relief just to know you're going somewhere there will be our kind of people. Be sure and change in time to answer the door. I don't want to have Alan see me in this shabby old dressing gown."

"Then why don't you change into something else?" Judith asked.

Millicent protested, "You know I'm not well!" And she hurried out.

Judith was only half finished with the task of hemming the dress and was glad to be left alone. Time was passing quickly, and she did want to be ready when Alan came for her.

He picked her up shortly before nine and gave her an admiring appraisal as he helped her into his car. "You look great!" was his comment.

She smiled. "I'm not sure I'm in a party mood."

"I never am until I get there," he said, turning on the ignition. "But Pauline always has interesting parties."

"I'm sure of it," Judith agreed, reaching to be sure she'd not upset her uplift hair-do when she'd gotten in the car. An examination showed it to be in place.

"We'll have the chance to meet a lot of people and get a cross-section of the town's opinions on the bridge crisis," he said, heading the car into a main street that would eventually lead them to the gallery.

"I've been hearing Mother's views for the past hour, and I've had my fill," Judith told him.

He laughed. "Were they that bad?"

"She's hopelessly mixed up about it, and there was no point wearing myself out trying to make it clear to her," Judith said. She smiled at him. "I wonder if Pauline will really be glad to see me at the party?"

"She invited you."

"She's a very generous person. That's why I feel a little awkward about us."

"Pauline told me to pick you up," he said. "She knew I wouldn't be calling for her. It gave me something to do."

Judith smiled at him. "I hope you'll be able to apply this same guile when it comes to dealing with Senator Lafferty."

"Which reminds me," Alan said, "you may see the Senator tonight. He often attends the gallery parties. He and his wife fancy themselves as art patrons."

"He should be able to buy a few paintings with all the graft he's collected," she said indignantly. "I don't know what I'll say if I meet him there!"

Alan laughed. "You won't have to say anything. He'll come straight over to you and bow from the waist and say, 'I've never seen you looking prettier, Miss Barnes.' It's his standard speech!"

"I've never seen you looking prettier, Miss Barnes," the Senator said with a bow, as he came across to join Judith in the crowded room. He glanced around with a smile on his bloated baby face, "I seem to have lost my wife, but who needs her with all you pretty girls around!"

Judith tried to hide her exasperation. The big gallery was noisy with the chattering of the various groups crowded into it. Scant attention was being paid to the display of paintings on the walls as the guests moved about with glasses in hand, greeting each other with shrill gaiety.

She forced a smile for the Senator and said, "I hardly expected you to be here. You're so busy presenting petitions these days."

"Public service, my dear," the pot-bellied man said pompously. "But I never let it interfere with my private amusements. Never!"

"Do you really think that extra spur should be added to the bridge?" she inquired with suitable innocence.

"It's a must, Miss Barnes," the Senator assured her. "And I have every reason to believe the Governor will agree."

She lifted her eyebrows. "Oh! You've already discussed it with him?"

Senator Lafferty looked disturbed. "Not at all! But we think along the same lines in such matters." He shifted his glance across the room. "I believe I see my wife. If you'll excuse me!" He offered another of his ridiculous bows and trotted off.

Judith watched him go, convinced that he hadn't rushed off to join his long-suffering wife but to get away from her. She had touched on a delicate subject, and he wasn't about to commit himself for her benefit.

She was left standing alone for a moment until Alan came pushing through the cluster of people to reach her. He looked exceedingly handsome in his dark suit, and he was wearing a confident smile.

"Everyone seems to be having a good time," he said.

"The Senator has just been entertaining me," she told him with an amused glance.

"Then you've been royally entertained," Alan said. "Did you get any dirt from him?"

"I started to dig, and he turned coward and ran off," she complained.

"That's our Senator!" Alan said. "Better luck another time."

"I'll be satisfied if he doesn't bother me for the rest of the evening," Judith said.

A slender, pale young man with very light yellow hair came strolling by and seeing Alan, offered him a languid smile. "Hi, Alan!" Next, glancing at Judith, he showed mild surprise and said, "And Judith!" It was none other than Charles North, the son of the famous S.C.

Alan said, "I guess everybody is here."

"I'd say so," Charles North agreed. "Pauline always has the best parties. Been a long time since I've seen you, Judith."

"Yes." She wasn't able to smile. Her feelings where Charles North was concerned had been too bitter since the incident involving Miles Estey. She couldn't stand him.

Now, with an insolence she hadn't believed possible, he asked casually, "Where's your old boy friend, Miles?"

Her eyes met his. "Don't you know?"

Charles North smiled nastily. "We've sort of lost track of him since he left the city in such a hurry."

Judith said, "Were you surprised that he went away?"

Charles North showed no uneasiness. "In a way," he said. "But then I guess he knew what was best for him."

"I thought it must have pleased you."

"Why should it?"

She shrugged. "I don't know. I just had that impression."

There was a hard expression in the young man's blue eyes. He said, "I don't expect he'll be back."

Judith said, "I imagine you'd be surprised if he did decide to return."

"It would be a very unwise move for him to make," Charles North said, a flush of anger mounting his pale cheeks.

Judith raised her eyebrows. "I wonder!"

Charles North turned his attention to Alan, saying, "Looks as if you're about to get a badly needed vacation, Alan. They're going to shut your bridge down."

"It hasn't happened yet," Alan told him.

"According to the papers, it's only a matter of a week or so," young North said with a mocking smile. "Harvey Wheaton won't have to worry any more about those overdue steel deliveries."

"It'll give us a chance to build a stock-pile," Alan suggested.

"But then you mightn't need one, might you?" North asked with another of his

140

smiles. Nodding to Judith, he said, "See you both later!" And he moved on.

"Now I know I shouldn't have come," Judith said with a despairing look at Alan.

"I don't agree," he told her. "We got him mad enough to tip his hand about the steel. There's no doubt that's what is bothering his father."

"You heard the way he sneered at poor Miles Estey!" Judith said.

"If what you think is true, it's exactly the way you'd expect him to talk," Alan reminded her. "We've got quite a cross-section of town to study tonight. Make the best of it."

Judith was beginning to weary of the crowd and the noisy conversation. Also, the room was becoming uncomfortably warm. As she and Alan stood chatting, they were interrupted by an art teacher friend of Pauline's. He was a hunched little man with a freaky black mustache and beard. He beamed at them from behind his horn-rimmed glasses and in a very British accent inquired if they'd seen the work of the featured artist.

"I'm afraid not," Judith said with a wan smile. "There's such a crush."

The bearded man nodded his head. "Don't I know it!" he said. And then, leaning forward confidentially, he said, "Don't worry about missing the display. It's very ordinary work! I've done much better myself."

"Well, at least you're modest," Alan teased him.

The art teacher shrugged. "One needn't be any more. It's very much the mod thing to be outspokenly frank. If one has talent, one should push oneself!" And suddenly seeing a crony in the distance, he raised a bony hand and, uttering a weird cry of recognition, hurried on.

"One is very hard to take," Judith told Alan wryly.

"A recent import from London," Alan informed her. "Considers himself a priceless addition to our local school system."

"It would be good to meet just one nice, friendly, ordinary human being here," Judith wailed.

Alan laughed. "Here comes one," he said. "Our hostess."

Pauline was wearing a gold spangled dress with the usual above the knee skirt. She came forward to join them with a pleasant smile on her attractive face. "At last!" she said with some sincerity. "Two of my favorite people, and together."

"The place is really rocking," Alan told

her. "It's the party of the year!"

"But will it sell any paintings?" Pauline asked with a grimace. "I'm beginning to wonder."

"They're bound to buy something just to make sure they get invited to your next binge," Alan assured her.

Pauline turned a laughing face to Judith. "I'm so glad you made up your mind to come."

"It's been fun," she said. "But isn't it getting warm?"

"I'm dying!" the girl in the gold dress said. "Alan, be a good fellow and see if you can get some air in this place." As he walked off, she turned to Judith and added, "I've been working to get ready for this since noon! I'm dead tired! Let's sneak off to my office for a few minutes of quiet. I need some rest before I face the leavetakings!" And she took Judith by the hand and led her through the crowded room to a door far at the back.

They went inside and down a short hallway to another door which led to a pleasantly furnished office with a desk, filing cabinet and several comfortable-looking chairs. It was brightly lit, with colorful blue drapes along one wall.

"Sit down," Pauline said, sinking into a

chair. "I must be out of my mind to try and entertain a mob like that."

Judith smiled. "If it helps business."

The other girl gave her a sharp look. "Speaking of business, what's going on about the bridge? I've hardly had a chance to look at the papers, but they seem to be criticizing my Alan roundly!"

"Alan is not in the wrong," Judith said firmly.

Pauline considered this as she lit herself a cigarette. Then she said, "I guess you should know." She held out the pack and lighter. "I should have offered you one first."

"Thanks; I don't smoke."

Pauline raised her carefully painted eyebrows. "No vices?"

"Smoking isn't one of them."

The other girl laughed as she leaned back in her chair and exhaled two spirals of smoke. "I've been dying for this. So you don't think Alan is in any trouble?"

"I didn't say that."

"Oh?"

Judith wasn't sure she liked Pauline's attitude. She seemed just a bit too casual. "I'm sure Alan will be anxious to explain all about it himself," Judith said, "just as soon as he has a chance."

Pauline flung her hand out in a gesture. "You know how introverted he is. I'll be lucky if I can drag anything out of him. That's why I'm asking you now."

"It's mostly politics and a power play," Judith said. "To put it very simply, the Senator is trying to prove that Alan had the bridge plans changed to elminate the North End spur without telling the public. That simply isn't true. Now the Senator is stirring up trouble to have the work on the bridge halted, Alan dismissed as chairman of the bridge authority or pressure exerted to force him to resign, and the steel contracts that are being filled by an out-of-state company turned over to the S.C. North mills, even though they're asking a ridiculous price." She paused briefly. "That's what it's really about. North wants the steel contracts."

Pauline had been listening with growing interest. "You make it sound as if they're out to get Alan."

"It seems they are."

"Do you think they will?"

Judith sighed. "It's too soon to know."

The girl in gold took a deep puff on her cigarette and then exhaled. "I think he ought to resign right away. He should never have gotten mixed up in that bridge thing."

"But it's given him responsibility and a lot of experience," Judith hastened to tell her. "He's gained a lot of it."

Pauline gave her a wry look. "So it seems."

"I mean until now," Judith faltered.

"The papers aren't treating him very kindly, from what I read."

"That's just been lately," she said. "It happens to almost everyone who is in the public eye. All the comments can't be favorable."

Pauline stared at her. "But from what you've said, I gather he's trying to fight S.C. North?"

"In a way."

The girl in gold looked astonished. "Hasn't he any better sense than that?"

"He believes he is right."

Pauline gave a small laugh. "Honey, S.C. North is Mr. Right in this town, and I mean always and every time."

"You'll have to discuss that with Alan."

"I intend to," the other girl said. "My father has S.C. North as his chief stockholder, and I can tell you we treat the name with proper respect in our house."

"I didn't know he owned part of the shoe company," Judith said. It was a revelation for her, another hint of how the octopus of the North interests had reached out to grasp control of nearly every big firm in the area.

"I don't think my father is going to be happy about Alan getting himself in this trouble," Pauline continued.

"It's the Senator and the North interests who are causing the trouble," Judith said; "not Alan."

"The way I see it, he's stuck his neck out and asked for it! My father will be in a rage! I know it!"

"Perhaps you had better explain your father's position to Alan," she said. "I doubt if he knows S.C. North is his silent partner any more than I did."

"The sooner the better," Pauline agreed. "You know Father didn't want me to get engaged to Alan."

"No?" Judith was embarrassed by the confidence.

"He considers him a kookie character, if you know what I mean," Pauline said frankly. "Sort of a sleepy Joe in his father's law firm. He hasn't ever done anything in a business way."

"He studied to be a lawyer."

"Sure," Pauline agreed. "And I say he has a lot of charm. I think he's really marvelous. You know that shy way he has! It really gets me."

"He is nice," Judith murmured weakly, devoutly wishing she was anywhere else, even back in the crowded room.

"Nice!" Pauline showed surprise. "Surely you can think of stronger adjectives than that! The Mayor is nice! Fred Harvey is nice! But that's not enough for my Alan. He's devastating in a kookie kind of way."

Judith managed a smile. "That's what I really meant."

"Sure you did," Pauline said. "Didn't you used to go with him once? I mean, you were like his steady girl friend?"

"We were quite close."

"Yes, close." Pauline eyed her warily. "That was before you met Miles Estey?"

She nodded. "Yes."

"Too bad about Miles," Pauline said with a sigh. "I'd never have taken him to be a thief!"

"I don't think he is," she said, rising quickly. "Don't you think we ought to be getting back to the others? They'll be missing you."

"You're right, darling!" Pauline stashed out her cigarette and got up. The girl in the gold dress added, "I hope I didn't hurt your feelings because of what I said about Miles Estey."

"It's all right," Judith assured her, leading

the way out, desperate to be rid of the other girl.

"I mean I want us to be good friends, I really do," Pauline said, coming down the dark hall after her. "Because of Alan, I think it's terribly important we like each other."

Judith said nothing, knowing it was much too late for that.

CHAPTER NINE

At long last the party was thinning out. The air was heavy with smoke, and there were still quite a few people left in the gallery, but it was no longer as crowded as before. Pauline left Judith to bid good night to some guests as soon as the two girls returned to the main gallery.

Judith stood alone for a moment debating how she'd get home. Then Alan came to join her once more. He was looking weary now. He smiled and said, "What do you say to leaving?"

"Won't you have to take Pauline home?"

"She'll be here for at least an hour or more. I'll come back for her. I'd say the interesting part of the evening was over."

"Yes. I'd like to go," Judith agreed quickly.

"Get your coat, and I'll meet you at the door," he said.

She quickly found the light summer coat she'd worn on the rack Pauline had set out in a corner and hurried across the room to meet Alan. Pauline was there seeing people on their way, and Judith quickly thanked her and said good night.

"I wish I could get away now, too," Pauline confided in her ear. "You're the lucky one." And to Alan: "I'll see you later, darling."

Alan gave her an affirmative nod, and Judith and he left. When they were alone in the car, she sank back on the cushion and gave a small moan of relief.

"What a night!" she gasped.

Alan laughed. "Don't complain! You've made the Port Winter scene."

"I could have done without it," Judith said.

"Well, at least you met a few interesting types."

"Senator Lafferty, Charles North and that creepy artist!" she said with disgust.

From the wheel Alan said, "At least you escaped for a while. Did you and Pauline have a girl to girl talk?"

"Yes." She knew her voice sounded dull; it reflected her mental state.

"You don't sound completely enthusiastic about it."

"I'm not."

He gave her a quick glance. "What happened?"

"Nothing," she said with a sigh. And then, turning to him in a burst of confidence, she said, "Alan, I hate to sound catty, but I've never talked much with Pauline until tonight. She's not exactly what I thought her to be."

"No?"

"Not at all! She's so shallow!"

He nodded, his eyes on the dark street ahead. "I've been trying to tell you that, but you wouldn't listen."

"I had such a different mental picture of her."

"Well, now you know," he said.

"I'll go further, since I've begun," she said, turning to him with sober eyes. "Whatever happens between us, I think you should break with her anyway. She's not right for you."

"I agree with everything but that 'whatever happens between us.' You know what's going to happen. We'll marry and live happily ever afterward."

"You've been reading too much Hans Christian Andersen," she told him lightly.

"Better fantasy than the real thing, if tonight is any example," Alan told her with a sigh. "I was given the third degree on all sides."

"I hate to say it," Judith warned him, "but

I think you're going to get more of the same."

"I am?"

"From Pauline."

"Oh, no!" he protested. "Are you sure?"

"She said as much when we had our talk just now."

"That caps it," Alan said unhappily. "I thought she was so wrapped up in her own affairs she wasn't even aware of my problems."

"It just got through to her. She feels you have a kind of shy kookie charm, and what she read about you in the newspaper didn't fill her cup with happiness."

"Why should she care?"

"She wants a charm boy with no involvements. She thinks you should resign and devote yourself to creating a life beautiful for her."

"It sounds dreadful!"

"She's willing to admit you know nothing about business and you haven't been what the Mayor would call 'a fast halfback' in law, but she's sure you have the ability to decorate her cocktail parties." Judith knew she sounded bitter, but she was so raging at the comments the other girl had made she couldn't help it.

Alan gave her a smile as they came to a

halt in front of her steps. "Well, at least you know now where my future lies."

"Get away from her," Judith advised, "and quick!"

"Just a short time ago you were advising me not to rush to break my engagement. I wish you'd make up your mind."

"It's made up where she is concerned," Judith told him. "She's well meaning, I guess, but I consider her a threat to you or any other man she takes under her protective wing."

"At least I've been warned."

"And another thing. She considers you crazy to buck the great S.C. North."

Alan registered surprise. "How did she come to mention him?"

"It seems he owns a major part of her father's shoe factory, and she has no desire to upset Daddy or S.C. North."

"Whew!" Alan gave a low whistle. "First I've heard about that. So S.C. has a mortgage on old man Walsh! What doesn't he own in this town?"

"You, I hope," she said sincerely.

"I guarantee it!"

"You'd better get back to Pauline," she said. "And, Alan, if you —" She let her voice trail off.

"I know," he said happily. "If I'm going to

kiss you good night, do it here in the car so your mother won't share our moment of bliss!" And with a soft laugh he gathered her in his arms for a long, meaningful kiss.

It was warm and sunny on Saturday morning, but rain had been promised for late afternoon or early evening. Millicent Barnes in her shabby wrapper hovered over the breakfast table hungrily, awaiting the details of the party from Judith.

Not until she was having her coffee could she summon enough energy and enthusiasm to give her mother an account of what now seemed to her a kind of nightmarish event. However, she tried hard not to disillusion her mother.

"The place was crowded," she said. "There was hardly room to move around."

Millicent Barnes sat across the table from her with a broad smile on her pale, wrinkled face. "I know the store. I used to shop there when I was a girl."

"Well, she's taken out all the partitions. It's just one big room now," Judith said. "She has her office at the back. It's small, but it's very nice."

"Were there a lot of beautiful paintings on display?" Her mother's eyes were bright.

Judith hedged. "Some of them were quite startling," she said. "You see Pauline is interested mostly in abstract and pop art."

"I know so little about modern art," her mother mourned. "I've gotten so out of touch."

"You haven't missed too much," Judith assured her. "Of course some of them were colorful. And there were plenty I couldn't begin to understand. People didn't pay too much attention to the art; they were mostly talking among themselves."

"And I'd have expected them to spend their time moving from painting to painting."

Judith restrained a smile and drank the balance of her coffee. As she put the cup down, she said, "I'm afraid they weren't that much interested."

Millicent sighed, happily determined to look on the bright side. "Well, at least you met a lot of fine people. You were associating with your own kind again. If you only knew how much that means to me."

Judith stared at her mother. "I had a long private chat with Pauline Walsh," she said.

"Now I'll bet she's grown into a charming girl," her mother said. "I've seen her pictures in the paper, and she always looks so stunning. Too bad she had that unhappy marriage. But then it's only too easy to marry the wrong man."

"I suppose so," Judith said vaguely, afraid of what her mother might say next.

Millicent didn't disappoint her. Staring mournfully down at her skinny hands, which she worked nervously, she said, "I often wonder what my life would have been like if I'd married someone other than your father. I'm sure things would have been different for me now."

Judith tried to keep the edge out of her voice. "You and Father were always happy as I remember it."

"But look how we were left!" She sighed. "My parents warned me, but I wouldn't listen. I thought I was in love."

Judith felt her face flush and looked down to avoid seeing the pitiful caricature of what had once been fragile beauty. She said, "Weren't you?"

There was a short pause. "Yes. I suppose I was for a while. But it didn't last. It didn't last nearly long enough."

She glanced up at the forlorn woman, trying desperately to hide her disapproval. "Does love ever last? I mean for anyone. Do you honestly think you were cheated more than others in your marriage? I don't think so!"

"Your father was a good man," Millicent said hastily. "He treated me like a child, but

I forgive him for that. But he wasn't of my background. For generations the Melroses have been looked up to in this town. I should have married one of my own kind. I could have found a husband in one of the other old families. But I was such a foolish girl. I had eyes for no one but your father." She paused and then with a coy smile added, "I've been thinking of what you said about Brandon Fraser asking for me the other day. I remember he showed a lot of interest in me when I was a girl. I'm sure I could have had him if I'd only half-tried."

Judith stared at her mother in disbelief. "You can't mean that seriously! From what I've seen of Brandon Fraser, I think you'd be a very unhappy person if you were married to him today."

"Well, I don't know." Millicent sighed. "We never hear much about his wife. Sarah has been an invalid with a private nurse for years now. It must be hard on him and on Alan."

"I'm sure it is," Judith agreed. "Alan doesn't talk about his mother, although he did say once she's not been mentally well since her stroke."

"I guessed that," Millicent said. "But the Frasers are such fine people, and so are the Walshes. I think it would be nice if you and that nice Pauline could become close friends."

Judith smiled at the irony of it. "That's what she told me last night."

"You see!" her mother said happily.

"But I can't be friends with her, Mother," Judith said angrily. "I don't care if she has blue blood trailing all the way back to the Mayflower; she's a silly, shallow person without a thought in her head." And she got up.

"You can say that after being a guest at her party last night?"

"I don't think that has anything to do with it," Judith said. "If Pauline is a sample of your best families, I can get along very well without them." And she started off to her room to dress.

Her mother's wail followed her. "Just like your father!"

In spite of the predicted rain, the day continued pleasant, with plenty of warm sunshine. Judith made peace with her mother and then went out to work in the garden.

She stayed there until late afternoon and then decided to clean up and take a stroll to the Public Gardens and the lake. There was a path circling the lake that wound its way among tall evergreens, slim white birches reaching to the sky, and wandered up and down rocky places in true woodland fashion.

Walking in the quiet of the woods broken only by the occasional loud cry of a bird from above, the flutter of wings or the scurrying of squirrels in the dry branches, she was able to give her thoughts full play. And as she made her way along the path this Saturday afternoon in early June, her mind was filled with the problems that had come crowding into her life during the past week.

She was so lost in her thoughts that when she came out into the open by a large boulder, at first she did not see the solitary figure standing gazing sullenly down at the lake far below. It took her a full moment to realize the man in the neat gray suit and straw hat was Brandon Fraser.

His surprise appeared to be equally great as he turned toward her. "Miss Barnes," he said, removing his straw hat and taking a step down from the rocks toward her.

She smiled. "You decided to take a walk on this lovely afternoon, too."

"Yes," he said, still ill at ease. "This is a favorite place of mine. I've been coming here for years. You like it as well?"

"I often come here, right up until the late autumn. I think it's even more beautiful when the leaves change color."

He stared at her with his deep-set eyes. "I wonder we haven't met here before."

"It along path," she said. "It goes completely around the lake. I hardly ever go all the way. It's possible for quite a few people to be strolling here at the same time and not meet each other."

Brandon Fraser nodded. "That's true," he agreed. He returned the flat-crowned straw hat to his head and turned to gaze out at the lake and some distant rowboats.

"Standing here, I sometimes get the impression time has stood still," he said. "Things are very much as they were when I was a boy. No crush of automobiles, no herds of people, nothing but the woods, the lake and a few boats."

"Life must have been much simpler and pleasanter then," she said.

"I like to think so," Brandon Fraser said. "But then my father used to tell me the same thing. And I suppose my grandfather complained about the great change since his day. We have to accept what the years bring us, good and bad." He looked at her with a cold smile. "Still, it is good to have a refuge."

"I'm convinced of that."

Still facing her, he said, "I'm afraid I

wasn't very pleasant to you in the office yesterday."

She looked out at the lake to avoid his gaze. "I didn't notice."

"That's polite but hardly honest."

Judith shrugged. "Perhaps I should have said it wasn't important to me."

"I hope that is true," Alan's father said in his precise voice. "I feel unhappy at the idea I might have given you a bad impression of myself."

Still studying the lake, she said, "I did feel sorry for Alan."

"I see," he said quietly. This was followed by a deep sigh. "I can't expect you to understand."

Now she turned to him. "I think I do," she said. "It's this fantasy you've built around Brian's memory that is causing you to hate Alan."

"You think that?"

"I know it's true."

Brandon Fraser's bony face worked with emotion. In a choked voice he reminded her, "But you knew Brian. You saw him many times. You surely realize what a fine young man he was!"

"I've told you I liked Brian," she said quietly.

"All that promise lost!"

"You're hurting yourself and Alan need-lessly," Judith told him. "It's useless to go on grieving for Brian this way."

The man opposite her shook his head. "Such a waste of life!"

"I'll grant that Brian might have had a wonderful future," she said. "But I know that he once told me he was worried about Alan."

Brandon Fraser stood very still. "Brian said that?"

"Yes. In fact, you were brought into the discussion. He felt that you were giving Alan some kind of complex by paying him such scant attention. And Brian was weighed down by the obligation to win in everything that you thrust on him. He was troubled by the partiality you showed him and, in return, the demands you made of him."

The deep-set eyes stared at her incredu-lously. "Brian talked about me that way. Told you, a stranger, of his deepest feel-ings?"

"I was hardly a stranger," she said. "We could have fallen in love, but I decided I cared more for Alan."

Brandon Fraser regarded her angrily. "How do I know you're not making all this up? He never said such things to me!"

"Because I think he feared you," Judith said, "just as I believe Alan feared you until yesterday. Your sons loved you, but their fear of your coldness made it impossible for them to tell you what they really thought. It's too late for Brian now. But I think Alan has learned to stand up to you."

He swallowed hard. "Then it was you who put him up to defying me," he said. "You filled him with the lies you've told me just now."

"If you're suggesting that I told him what Brian said to me, I did." Judith faced Alan's father with the knowledge that this was something that must be endured. "I felt it might help him. And I believe it was of some value."

Brandon Fraser stood staring at her in silence for at least several minutes longer, his gaunt face completely expressionless. Then he wheeled around abruptly and walked away. She watched him vanish in the woods with mixed feelings. She would have preferred to have avoided the scene that had been forced on her, and yet she was grateful that she'd had a chance to say what she had kept to herself for so long.

She finished her walk in solitude. And by the time she took the road back home she was in a relaxed mood again.

A brisk ten-minute walk brought her back to Mount Pleasant and the rows of fine old homes built on the hills overlooking the city. She hoped she would be able to earn enough to keep their house. It was her mother's last link with the great days of her family. And although they could have lived much less expensively in an apartment and it would have been more practical if they had been in a more central location where she wouldn't need to depend on bus transportation, she had no intention of making a change unless necessity demanded it.

She passed the mansion of S.C. North set in a good distance from the road and surrounded by many acres of estate. The financier was hardly ever there, traveling most of the time, looking after his many enterprises. A short distance farther on, she came to the Fraser home, a stately brick with less impressive grounds, but commanding a fine view of the harbor and the East End of the city.

Her own home was ahead and on the right. Because of its location on a hill, there were all those concrete steps to mount. Not a house for the aged or the arthritic, she decided with a smile.

She was just about to start up the steps when she realized a car had come up behind her and stopped. She turned to see who it might be. The blue sedan was not familiar, but when its door opened and the driver stepped out, he was! It was Miles Estey come back!

CHAPTER TEN

"Miles!" she exclaimed in a startled voice.

"I saw you coming down the street," he said with a smile.

Judith stared at him, and her immediate reaction was that he had aged in the short time since she'd seen him. The tall, sturdy young man's pleasant face had a new maturity. But the red hair was as vivid as ever, and he seemed in excellent physical condition. He wore a neat dark suit.

"I had no idea you were in town," she said.

"I just got here."

"It's good to see you again. Are you staying or just passing through?"

He continued to study her with those keen blue eyes until she felt embarrassed. "I'll be here for a while," he said.

"I wondered why I didn't hear from you."

Miles gave her one of his familiar smiles. "Didn't I send you a Christmas card?"

"Without a message or an address," she said. "That was hardly enough."

"I wasn't sure it still mattered to you."

"You know better than that! Several times

I've wanted to write you and didn't have any address."

Miles said, "I'd like to talk to you."

She glanced up toward the house, wondering if her mother was looking out.

"Perhaps we could meet later. After dinner."

"Suits me," he said. "I haven't checked in at my motel yet. Suppose I come by around eight?"

Thinking quickly, she realized it wouldn't be dark by then. So she said, "Why not make it around nine-fifteen?"

"If you like," he agreed in a casual tone, so casual she had an idea he knew why she'd suggested a later time.

"My mother takes too much interest in my business," she said by way of explanation. "It would be better if I came out to meet you rather than have you call for me."

"Why not?" he asked in the same bantering tone.

She glanced at him anxiously. "Miles, please understand this is nothing personal. I have to cope with her this way all the time. Otherwise she worries and is miserable."

Miles offered her a lopsided grin. "I'll buy anything you say."

"Don't be like that!" she said, more aware now of the new hardness in him, the cynicism and distrust that apparently extended even to her.

"I'll be here as soon as it's properly dark," he said. "In the meantime, I'll be on my way before all the neighbors see me talking to you."

"Miles!" she reproved him.

But he was already moving around to the other side of his car to get into it. He waved in a friendly fashion, but the smile he assumed was bitter. She watched with a sinking heart as he started the car and drove away. He had changed!

She entered the house, expecting her mother to pounce on her with a tirade because she'd been talking with Miles. But it turned out she was in luck. Millicent was still in her room, finishing an afternoon nap. Judith drew a deep sigh of relief and prepared to offer her mother a story to cover her going out with Miles later.

She waited until after dinner and then, pretending it had just occurred to her, said, "I forgot. I promised to go to the Yacht Club dance with Alan."

Millicent smiled with pleasure. "Well, you're certainly late thinking about it. What are you going to wear? Is it a formal?"

"No. The season hasn't started yet. This is only an informal affair to bring the members together and discuss plans and enjoy some dancing. I'll just wear something simple."

"You don't want to look out of place," her mother worried.

"That's why I'll not wear anything dressy," Judith said firmly. "I can put on my blue. It's new and will be suitable."

By nine o'clock she was ready. The rain hadn't started, and so she made an excuse she wanted to enjoy some fresh air before Alan picked her up. Then she hurried down to the sidewalk to wait for Miles. She took a stand a short distance from the house and near a street lamp. He arrived at exactly nine-fifteen.

He gave her a teasing smile as she got in beside him. "Hope I didn't keep you waiting?"

"No. I just came down."

"I trust you gave your mother a suitable story."

"Don't be difficult, Miles," she begged. "It doesn't become you."

He glanced at her. "Any place special you want to go?"

"Not really," she said. "Why don't we drive to the Point? It's only a few miles from town, and there's a lot of parking space overlooking the beach and river. And on the way back we can stop at the Ranch House for a snack. We often used to do that."

"Sounds good," he said, heading the car down the hill to the bridge and the rotary leading to the Point road.

Judith sat back with a sigh of relief. "I can hardly believe you're back," she said.

He didn't take his eyes from the wheel. "Did you think I wouldn't dare?"

"Of course not! But I'd had no word from you."

Miles eased the car into the heavy flow of traffic circling in front of the Holiday Inn and took the exit for the Point road. "I didn't know until a short time ago I'd be coming here. I decided to keep it a surprise."

"It has been one!"

He drove on without glancing at her. "A pleasant one, I hope."

"Of course!" She sensed that he was still in a hostile humor and wanted to get him out of it. "You're looking very well. I've been worried about you."

"Thanks. But I've managed."

"What are you doing?"

He gave a short laugh. "I think I've finally found my proper niche. You know I was never happy working here for North."

"I know."

"And I didn't really care much for accountancy. So when I had my trouble, I decided I should investigate other fields."

"And you found something you liked?"

"Yes. I'm with one of the big labor unions. Sort of a trouble-shooter and organizer."

Judith turned to him. "That's wonderful," she said sincerely. "I'm sure you'll do well." And then it hit her! "Is that why you're here?"

"That's right," he said with irony.

"Miles, you've not come about the bridge, have you? I understand they plan some kind of demand for new working conditions."

"I'm here to look after the interests of the bridge workers," he admitted. And giving her a side glance for the first time, he asked, "Does that make me any less welcome?"

"Not you as a person," she said faintly. And then she admitted, "But you have arrived at the worst possible time. You must know that Alan Fraser is fighting a battle with Senator Lafferty to prevent the construction from being halted completely."

"Their political battles don't concern me," Miles said bluntly. "I'm only concerned with getting the best possible conditions for our men when they are working."

"I can understand that," she said. "But your coming here with a strike threat at this particular moment will make it more difficult for Alan!"

Miles eyed her sardonically. "You sound very worried about Fraser!"

"I'm his secretary now," she explained. "I've worked with him closely all through this. He's put an awful lot of effort into the bridge."

"The privileged son of a privileged father," Miles said coldly. "I'm sorry I can't work up much enthusiasm for the Port Winter gentry."

"Because Charles North played a rotten trick on you is no reason you should condemn everyone in town," she protested.

"I don't care about the precious town," he told her. "It doesn't happen to be my town any more. I've been sent here to do a job, and that's what I'm taking care of no matter who gets hurt."

"You're playing into S.C. North's hands," Judith warned him. "He's out to remove Alan from the bridge authority and hold up construction until he can have his own men placed in charge and the steel contract shifted to him. Senator Lafferty is merely fronting for the North interests."

They had reached the Point, and Miles

brought the car to a halt facing the beach. The canteen was open, and there was a scattering of cars, but the dark threatening night had made the number smaller than would have been present on a moonlit night.

Miles turned off the ignition and stared up at the dark sky. "I'd say that rain wasn't far away."

She stared at him with troubled eyes. "Are you deliberately trying to hurt Alan?"

He turned. "I'm not interested in Alan. Get that? And I'm not interested in any of these local squabbles. I'm here to represent the workers. That's it!"

"Miles, you've changed terribly!"

"Meaning I'm no longer an easy mark?"

"Meaning you've become hard and mean. You mustn't go on this way! It's as if you were a different person, someone I don't know!"

"I am a different person! Do you think I had an easy time getting started again? Do you think anyone worried about me? The Norths taught me a lesson that I'm not apt ever to forget. I hope I can go on putting it to good advantage."

"You've come back here hoping to cause trouble."

"If you're saying I don't mind if someone gets hurt, you're right. I was hurt, and I know what happened. The people of this town turned their backs on me. I thought I had friends until North told them I was a thief!"

"I never believed it," she said in a tense whisper. "You know that!"

"Maybe you didn't," he said. "But you were still nervous talking to me today where the neighbors might see you. And you had to lie to your mother to come out with me tonight! I don't call that taking a strong stand in the accused's defense."

"You're twisting everything to suit your own point of view," she protested. "I told you I always have trouble with Mother."

"Don't try to spare my feelings," Miles said sharply. "And don't go on pleading for Alan Fraser. I'm doing my job, regardless of how much it embarrasses him. I take it you and he are going together again, now that you're his secretary. He used to be your boy friend, as I remember."

"Do I have to answer that?" she asked with a hint of scorn.

"Forgive me if I've broken a code," Miles mocked her. "I know how strongly you Port Winter gentry adhere to your codes. But I believe in saying what I think."

She looked out at the river. "I told you I was glad you'd come back. That was a mistake. Now I'm sorry that you have. And I'm sorry for you."

"Thanks!"

"I mean it," she said, turning to him.

"I can take care of myself."

"I hope so," she said quietly.

Miles studied her in silence for a moment. Then he said, "No more pleading for your boy friend? You disappoint me."

"That wasn't why I came out with you tonight: to plead for Alan."

"I thought it was."

"I didn't even know you were working for the union when I asked you to pick me up."

He smiled bleakly. "I thought maybe somebody had given you a hint."

"They hadn't."

"In which case I offer an apology. So you wanted to see me tonight because you are still my good friend, because you still care for me."

"That's true in a way."

"Don't talk nonsense you don't mean. We were finished as soon as I was branded a thief."

"Perhaps it would have been impossible for us to go on in this town," she admitted. "But we could have gone some place else and made a fresh start together. You preferred to leave without telling me."

"I did what I considered best for both of us."

"You might have been wrong."

Miles lost his harshness for the first time. Very quietly he said, "It is cruel of you to say a thing like that unless you mean it."

"I do mean it."

Miles took her in his arms. "I shouldn't believe you," he said. "But I want to." And pressing her tightly to him, he kissed her hard. In a moment he let her go. "It's no use, Judith. We can't go back to what we had."

She said, "You seem very certain of that."

"Too many obstacles," he said with a wry smile. "For one thing, you're right. I have changed."

"Not that much."

"Enough," he said firmly. "I'm not even interested in being the kind of person I was before. I've found the meaning of power. And I've learned how to use it. With a little luck, I can go to the top in this game."

"Is that what you want?"

"I think so. I see our leaders as about as honest as S.C. North; maybe a little more so."

"Good luck, then."

"I'll need it," he said frankly. "They know about my record, and they've been willing to give me a chance. But I'll be watched for a while." He paused. "So Alan is the top man in your life again?"

She gave a rueful laugh. "I like the way you say again. I'm very fond of Alan. He's engaged to someone else at the moment."

Miles showed surprise. "I didn't expect that."

"I'll be honest," she said. "I think he's going to break his engagement. And I feel he should, both for his sake and the girl's. Also, he's asked me to marry him."

"That sounds more like it."

"I haven't promised that I would."

"Why?" Miles asked with one of his hard smiles. "Are you waiting to be sure he's a winner? Afraid he'll fall down on this bridge project? Holding off for a better prospect?"

"You have become cynical," she said quietly. "No. I didn't put him off for any of those reasons. I did it because of a lingering fondness for you."

"Me?"

"Yes. I wasn't certain I'd gotten over you. I'm not sure yet."

Miles said nothing for a moment. It was his turn to stare out across the river silently. Then he said, "It's beginning to rain. I see drops on the windshield. We'd better start back and have our snack. I don't want to keep you out too late."

"Whatever you think," she said listlessly. She turned to look out the side window and kept her head averted for a good part of the drive into the city.

The Ranch House was a log cabin restaurant on the outskirts of the city. Most of the time it featured folk singers as entertainment, and the menu consisted chiefly of various cuts of charcoal broiled steaks and lobster. It drew a mixed patronage, and when they entered on this Saturday night, it was well-filled and the show was under way. A waiter led them down an aisle of the nearly dark restaurant to the background accompaniment of twanging guitars and a sad-voiced male and female duo.

Miles glanced across the table with its flickering candle in a bottle covered with wax drippings and, smiling, said, "Seems like old times!"

She nodded. "We used to come here a lot."

They ordered and then listened to the folk singers, each lost in his own thoughts. Judith was almost glad the evening was coming to an end. The tension between herself and the young man to whom she'd once been engaged had been so great she knew they'd made each other unhappy.

When the show ended and the lights were turned on, Miles glanced around at the occupants of the adjacent stalls. "I don't see any familiar faces," he said.

"It's been a little while," she reminded him. "It doesn't take long for the crowd to change."

"You're right," he agreed.

They quickly finished their food, and Miles drove her back home. When the moment came for them to part, he showed his first sign of genuine regret.

"I suppose you'll not want to see me again," he said.

"Why do you say that?"

"This evening wasn't much of a success. And you don't approve of my reason for coming back to Port Winter."

"Let's not argue," she suggested with a smile. "I think we should see each other again."

"All right," he said. "I'll be in touch." And with another of his wry smiles: "I'll probably see you in your office. I'll be calling on Fraser."

"I'll be expecting you," she said.

He nodded and sighed. "Maybe we can talk it all out another time," he said. And leaning across, he kissed her briefly. Then he got out of the car and saw her to the steps.

She waited until he drove away, then, with a strangely depressed feeling, slowly started up the concrete steps.

Tonight her mother was waiting in the darkness of the living room. She saw the thin figure in the faded wrapper lift herself from an easy chair and come out to greet her. Her mother's pale face was expressionless.

"You're home from the dance early," she said.

"Alan didn't want to stay late," Judith told her. "We were both tired after last night."

Millicent stared at her bleakly. "Yes. I expect you would be."

"Are you feeling well?" Judith asked her mother anxiously. "You look so pale. You should go to bed and not wait up for me."

"You think not?"

"I think it's a lot of nonsense."

Millicent Barnes sighed. "You would. By the way, you had a phone call a little while after you left."

Judith was mildly surprised. "Oh? I wasn't expecting any."

"I realize that," her mother said with a touch of anger. "It was Alan Fraser who called. He asked that you call him back tomorrow."

Judith stood motionless and silent.

Finally she said, "I'm sorry, Mother."

"Well, you might be!" Millicent Barnes raged. "Going off with someone and telling me the first story that came into your head. Do you know what I've gone through since that call came?"

"There was no need to worry!" Judith protested.

"What would you expect me to do? And why did you lie to me in the first place?"

Judith wanted no more evasions. She had gotten herself in enough trouble as it was. She said, "I lied to save you from worry, Mother. I don't normally do it, but this was a special instance."

"Indeed!" Millicent said bitingly.

"Miles Estey is back in town," Judith went on. "He asked me to go out with him so we could have a talk. I knew you'd be upset, so I told you I was meeting Alan."

"Miles Estey!" Her mother's tone indicated how she felt about the young man.

"You needn't say his name that way," Judith told her angrily.

"You're going to start running around with him again just when Alan Fraser is getting interested in you!"

"You're being silly!"

"That's what you always say! But I guess I know who the silly one is this time! Turning your back on a nice boy like Alan to run after a thief!"

"Don't say that, Mother!" Judith warned her. "I'll see Miles whenever I like."

"Of course you will! You proved that to-night with your lies," Millicent said, beginning to sob. "It could be your father, you sound so much like him!"

"Mother!" Judith begged. And with a small moan of despair, she turned and ran down the hall to the refuge of her own room.

The rain came on Sunday. It poured down and suited Judith's mood. At breakfast she came to terms with her mother and tried to explain there was nothing to worry about in Miles Estey's return. Her mother was in one of her quiet, apathetic moods and it was hard to know whether Judith had made the situation plain to her or not.

Around noon she phoned Alan Fraser and was fortunate enough to get him on the line at the first try. He sounded glad to hear from her. "I called you last night," he said. "But I guess I just missed you."

"I went out for a little while," Judith said.

"I wanted to tell you," Alan continued, "that we have new troubles in the offing. A union organizer has just arrived in town."

"Oh!" she said, not wanting to commit herself.

"It could mean trouble. Not that it may make too much difference, since we have all we can handle anyway."

"Perhaps it won't turn out too badly," she ventured.

"I wouldn't count on that," he said, "especially since the union man happens to be someone who hasn't too much good will toward Port Winter. His name is Miles Estey."

"Miles," she repeated.

"I don't expect you to sound surprised," Alan went on dryly. "Someone told me they saw you with him at the Ranch House last night."

CHAPTER ELEVEN

Judith wasn't surprised to hear that she and Miles had been seen. In spite of the fact they hadn't noticed anyone they knew in their particular area of the restaurant, it was a big place and there had undoubtedly been people who had seen them coming in whom they hadn't seen.

Quickly recovering her poise, she said, "He got in touch with me as soon as he arrived in town."

"That's logical," Alan said, showing no sign of annoyance. "What kind of a mood is he in?"

"He's a lot different," she warned him. "There were times when I felt I was talking to a stranger."

"I see," Alan said quietly. "Did he mention his business here?"

"Yes. He's determined to get the workers a better deal."

"Does he know they may be facing a full lay-off?"

"That didn't seem to interest him."

There was a distinct sigh from the other end of the phone. "Well," Alan said, "I guess that is that."

Judith said, "Perhaps you can get somewhere with him when you meet."

"I'm going to call his motel right away," Alan said. "I hope I can arrange a meeting with him tonight; see him and get some idea what his demands are going to be."

"That could be a good idea," Judith agreed. "I wish you luck."

"I can use some," Alan said grimly. "I expect to get the final report on the shareholders of the plaza in the morning. I'm crossing my fingers that the Senator's name will be among them."

"It would simplify things," Judith said. "What about the housing project?"

"I've been too busy tracing the shopping center setup to go into it yet."

"I'll see you in the morning then," she said.

After she hung up, she went back to sit in the quiet of her own room and watch the rain beat down. She wondered if Alan would be successful in setting up a meeting with Miles and, if so, how the two would get along. It was odd that the two men who had figured in her life so prominently should now find themselves on opposing sides where the bridge was concerned.

She tried to picture their meeting and the

attitudes of each of the men. There was no doubt that Alan would try to be fair with the workers, but with his own authority in jeopardy at the moment, it was doubtful if he was in a very strong bargaining position. She was certain Miles would work for important gains for the union men he was representing, but she also felt he would be reasonable.

Surely the differences between union and management could be settled favorably in this instance. As she saw it, the big danger looming from the bridge was the threat offered by Senator Lafferty and his backers. Alan would have to come up with something strong to defeat them.

She believed that Alan would either prove himself in this crisis or go down to a personal defeat that might really blight his future. His father was to blame for many of Alan's personality faults and would bear a heavy share of the guilt if Alan failed. The face of the elder Fraser still haunted her following her confrontation with him on the woodland path. Brandon Fraser was a cold, bigoted man and surely a very unhappy one.

The day became evening without the rain letting up. And when she finally got into bed, it was still raining. It had been a dull, gray day filled with dark forebodings for the week ahead.

Alan was already in his office when she arrived the next morning. It was still gray and unpleasant, but the rain had ended. He glanced up with a smile when she came in.

"Ready for the big week?" he wanted to know.

Judith slipped off her raincoat, hung it up and patted her hair. Then she asked, "How did you make out with Miles Estey?"

"We had a meeting."

"With good results, I hope."

Alan shrugged. "You were right. He is in a tough mood. But I finally worked out a deal with him I think will be satisfactory to the bridge authority."

"You'll be calling them together at once, I suppose."

"That will be your first job this morning," Alan said briskly. "We'll meet at the City Hall at eight-thirty tonight. Call everyone and tell them it's urgent they be there."

She smiled. "Will Miles be meeting with them as well?"

"You can mention he'll be there," Alan said, "and also some representative members of the union. We've still got to come to an agreement on safety measures. I hope we can reach a compromise on them."

Judith sat down at her desk and kept busy on the phone for more than an hour. As she was calling bridge authority members she heard Alan busy on the other line following up the shopping center information. And by the time she finished and went into his office again, he had sheets of written notes spread out before him.

Glancing up at her, he asked, "Did you reach everyone?"

"Yes. And they all promised to be there," she said. "I think they're curious to find out what you're planning as a counter move to the Senator."

Alan looked grim. "Right this minute I wouldn't like to say we have anything to fight him with. He's clean as far as the shopping center is concerned."

Judith felt real disappointment. "Nothing to tie him in with it at all?"

"Nothing!" He frowned at the scribbled notes. "I've exhausted every source of information."

"Then we'll have to hope he may be connected with the housing development," Judith said.

"We'll start on that now," he promised. "It's essential we get the information before tonight's meeting if we can. I'll give you some numbers and the facts I'm looking for."

The morning passed quickly, but not much headway was made. Judith talked to the company acting as agents for the housing development, and they seemed to have little to offer about the financial backing of the building company. Further calls to subcontractors only brought the information that they had all dealt with one agent. She seemed to be getting nowhere.

Alan had little better luck. The bank handling the mortgages for the firm supplied him with the incorporation information and the listed officers. Of course Senator Lafferty's name was not included. Next, it was a matter of talking to these men and getting as much information as possible. Alan found them very tight-lipped. To all intents and purposes, the owners of the development were a trio of Italian brothers who had previously built several other similar developments with modest success.

The lunch hour came and went. Judith considered the fact that the senior Fraser had not made any appearance in his son's office. She couldn't help speculating on what his reaction had been to her lecture and wonder if it would make any change in his behavior toward Alan in the future. At

190

least he had not made his usual bullying call.

A few minutes after two, the door to Judith's office opened and a smiling Councilman Fred Harvey came in. The little man beamed at her behind his heavy-framed glasses, looking his usual immaculately neat self in a brown suit.

"How goes the battle?" he asked in his high-pitched voice.

"Grim," she said. "How was Washington?"

The bright eyes twinkled. "Profitable! Only trouble is that the train trip takes too long."

Judith laughed. "That problem is easy to solve. Switch to using planes instead."

"I detest flying," the little man said. "I'd rather suffer along with the ground transportation available."

"Don't say I didn't try to help." She nodded toward the closed door to Alan's office. "He's on the phone. I'll tell him you're here as soon as he finishes. Why don't you sit down?"

Councilman Fred Harvey continued to stare at her in his shrewd fashion as he settled in a nearby chair. "I hear you have a friend visiting town."

"You soon get caught up on local

gossip," she told him.

"I have my listening posts," he said with a chuckle. "It's only once in a long while they let me down."

Judith gave him a teasing glance. "I hear you've got both the Mayor's office and Senator Lafferty's bugged. Is that the truth?"

This tickled the little man. He chortled with glee. "If I did have a microphone hidden in either of those places, you don't think I'd tell you?"

"I'm sure you wouldn't," she said. "I think this bugging thing is the most unethical practice I've ever heard of. Imagine having all the transactions in an office down on tape and cold-bloodedly playing it back to steal information."

Fred Harvey shrugged. "Some of the biggest firms are using those things."

"Then I say the biggest firms are proving themselves to be pretty small," Judith told him.

At this point in their conversation Alan emerged from the inner office. "I thought I heard you out here," he said. "Smart of you to absent yourself from town while the Senator and his crowd had a Roman holiday taking pot shots at me."

The councilman smiled. "You look in pretty good shape in spite of it."

"I'm engaged in a last-ditch battle. Any ideas to help me?"

The alert eyes behind the horn-rimmed glasses fixed on him. "I gave you my advice before I went to Washington. If you can't beat them, why not join them?"

"Because they wouldn't have me, for one thing!" Alan said.

Fred Harvey winked. "Don't be too sure. I can still pull a few strings. I put you up for chairman; maybe I can keep you in the job."

"And maybe not! You don't know how North's newspaper has been tearing into me. They've accused me of everything but stealing and played up the overdue deliveries of steel just as you'd expect."

"They turn the water on, and they can turn it off," the little councilman said calmly. "One word from North, and the newspaper will start saying nice things about you again."

"And the union is after me as well. Their man arrived while you were away," Alan said.

"Miles Estey," Fred Harvey said with a chuckle. "I didn't expect to see him in Port Winter again."

"He's very much here," Alan said. "And he means business."

"You can deal with him if you settle with

the Senator," Fred Harvey suggested.

"I've been trying to do just that," Alan told him. "Judith and I have been on the phone all morning. The Mayor tossed us the idea. He thinks if we could prove the Senator has some tie-in with the shopping plaza or the housing development behind it, we could turn the tables on him; let the public see that he's trying to promote his own finances instead of their good."

The little man considered this. "Not a bad angle," he agreed.

"But not good enough," Alan complained. "We've exhausted every source, and there's nothing we can find to involve that bloated crook with either the shopping center or the development. We just can't dig up any proof!"

"I don't believe you'll ever get it," was Fred Harvey's opinion. "I tell you, Alan, my idea is the best. Let me see if I can't fix up a deal with the Senator."

Alan frowned. "What kind of deal?"

"He gets his North End spur, and you remain on as chairman of the bridge authority."

Alan was silent for a moment. "You don't think there's any honest way out of this?"

"If there is, it's escaped me," Fred Harvey

assured him. "And I have a reputation for being sharp."

"You're asking me to stop battling North and sell out to him! How can you be so sure the Governor will go along with his idea?"

Fred Harvey looked wise. "The Governor is worried about the coming election. He needs North's support and campaign contribution."

Alan's eyes narrowed. "I never expected to hear anything like this from you," he said. "Never expected you'd throw anything North's way."

"I don't want to do it," the little man said seriously. "Nor do I want to sacrifice you. I'm willing to compromise to bring you through this without a loss of reputation."

"What kind of a reputation will I have if I sell out?" Alan asked.

Fred Harvey stood up. "I'd say North's papers can do a pretty smart clean-up job on you, make you look so good you might be in line for some other important office when you're through with the bridge."

Alan stared at him. "Is that your last word?"

"It's the best I can do," Fred Harvey said, beaming happily again. "I know how you feel about this mess. But think it over, and I'm certain you won't think my offer is too bad. Just don't take too long to make up your mind. I'll have to talk to the Senator soon if you're to be salvaged."

Alan's thin sensitive face was the color of milk as Councilman Fred Harvey wished them a jaunty good afternoon and left. He remained standing there staring at the door for several minutes and then turned slowly to Judith. She was shocked by his expression of defeat. And she thought to herself, This is it! The crisis has reached its peak! This is where he turns and runs!

"You heard what he said?" Alan asked.

"I couldn't very well help it."

He shook his head. "And this is the man who backed me for the bridge job, the one who actively campaigned so that I got it!"

"I don't understand his attitude," Judith confessed.

Alan seemed not to have heard her. He was staring straight ahead. "All I have to do is shut up and buckle down to the Senator and North, and I get to remain the big man behind the bridge. It's all so simple!"

Judith said, "For once Fred Harvey must be on North's team. He must have something to gain by this."

Alan gave her a grim smile. "You're catching on! You're beginning to get it! Just a little more time associating with the right people, and we'll be old pros like the rest of them." He paused. "I know now why I was picked for chairman. Dad was right!"

Judith was becoming more alarmed every minute, sure that he was about to follow his usual pattern and retreat. "In what way?" she asked.

"I'll tell you," he said, pacing up and down and talking at the same time. "Why do you think Harvey picked me out of all the more likely candidates to head the bridge authority?" Without waiting for her to reply, he went on, "Because they wanted a strong man? A leader!" He stopped and shook his head. "No. They decided on me for the job because they wanted someone weak."

"You can't be sure of that," she protested.

"I am sure of it," he said. "They wanted a pushover, someone they could maneuver when the right time came." He sighed. "And it seems the time has come."

She was shaken by his self-condemnation. Getting up, she went to him and touched his arm. "You can't blame yourself! They've simply put you in an intolerable position. Harvey is the one most guilty."

"My own stupidity," he said, "my ego, got me into this. No wonder Dad opposed it from the beginning."

"Your father wasn't any more right than the rest of us," she hurried to say.

Alan shook his head. "Even Pauline had a little lecture prepared for me. Her father thought I should stay in line and mind my manners with Mr. S.C. North."

"North has been trying to get at you in every way possible."

"It seems he's done an excellent job as usual," Alan said with a bitter smile. "When I'm through with this, I won't even have my self-respect left."

"There has to be some way," Judith insisted. And as a last measure, she said, "Shouldn't you let the Mayor know what's been happening?"

He nodded. "Call him and see if he can come over. And tell him if he has any other helpful suggestions, they'll have to be better than the last ones." And he went into his own office and closed the door.

It took her quite a few minutes to locate the Mayor and then get him on the line. "It's Judith," she said. "We're in pretty bad trouble here. I wish you could come by."

"Any luck with your digging?" Mayor Jim Devlin wanted to know.

"None."

"That's too bad." The Mayor sounded

concerned. "I'll get there as soon as I can."

Alan was still shut up in his office when the Mayor arrived. The breezy Jim Devlin looked less assured and definitely worried. His stern face shadowed by fatigue, he glanced at the closed door to Alan's office and asked her, "Is he about ready to quit?"

"It doesn't look good," she said. Getting up, she knocked on the door and opened it to announce, "The Mayor is here."

Alan said, "I'll be right out." He joined them and quickly filled the Mayor in on the talk he'd had with Councilman Fred Harvey.

When he'd finished, the Mayor looked astonished. "I've never known Fred Harvey to play North's game before!"

"They must be working together this time," Alan said.

"Or he has some reason for wanting North to win," Mayor Jim Devlin pointed out. "And there's one other possibility. He feels responsible for you and he's trying to help you."

"If that's it, I'm not flattered," Alan said grimly.

"You've exhausted all the possibilities of connecting Lafferty with the shopping center or the housing development?" the Mayor asked.

"He's clean there," Alan said.

The Mayor rubbed his chin and stared ahead thoughtfully. "There must be some angle. I'm positive of it. What about Harrigan Street?"

"What about it?" Alan wanted to know.

"The entire street and all the buildings adjoining it will have to be razed if the North End spur becomes a reality," the Mayor said. "Now one building and lot wouldn't be worth much. But put them all together, and they would add up to a lot of money."

Judith saw what the Mayor was suggesting. She said, "You're wondering if there has been any big turnover in real estate in that area lately!"

"Exactly!" the Mayor said, his face lighting up. "It gives us another possible area of self-interest."

Alan shook his head. "It's a long shot."

The Mayor's eyes held their normal bright twinkle again. "But long shots invariably pay the best odds!"

His enthusiasm was catching, Alan hesitated only a few seconds. "I guess it's worth a try. But it'll mean a lot more digging than before. This time we'll have to look up deeds to almost half a hundred private properties. It can't be done in a day."

"But if we find what we're looking for, it will be worth it," Judith said, happy at the thought.

Alan glanced at his wristwatch. "Too late to begin now. The Registry of Deeds office will be closing in a few minutes. We'll have to start all over again first thing in the morning."

"Tell you what," the Mayor said. "I'll let you have a man from my office. There's an old fellow in the tax division knows that area better than anyone else at City Hall. I'll send him up to the deeds office to work with you."

Alan offered a faint smile again. "I hope you're not starting us on another wild chase for nothing!"

The Mayor winked. "I have a hunch! Let's follow it through."

As usual, he left them in much better spirits than when he'd arrived. Judith was faintly hopeful, although she didn't want to see Alan get too encouraged and then crash again as he had earlier in the day.

Alan said, "Since you've got to attend the authority meeting with me you may as well stay in the city, and we'll have dinner together. Then we can come back here and pick up what we need for the meeting."

She called her mother and explained. Millicent sounded doubtful, and Judith was waiting for her to make some comment about Miles Estey, but she didn't. She and Alan went across to the Harbor Room and had dinner. Since they had to hurry through the meal to return to the office and prepare notes for the meeting, they had little time to talk.

It was a few minutes after seven when they entered the office again. Alan found the minutes of the previous meeting, and they went to work on their program for the evening ahead. By working without a pause, they had everything in order by a few minutes before eight and were ready to leave for City Hall.

Alan smiled at her as he helped her on with her coat. "I haven't said anything before, but I will now. Thanks for the support you gave me today."

"I didn't feel I was much help," she demurred.

He swung her around and, taking her by the arms, looked into her face with great earnestness. "I dropped pretty low this afternoon. It would have been a lot worse if you hadn't been here."

"Then I'm glad I was."

"One thing worries me," he said, his eyes meeting hers.

"What?"

"Can I always depend on you being around?"

She smiled. "What makes you think I mightn't be?"

"Miles Estey is back in town."

"That's finished."

"You sound very sure of that."

"I am sure."

He shook his head. "You forget I spend last evening with him."

"So?"

"I don't think it's finished as far as he's concerned," Alan told her. "He had a certain note in his voice every time he mentioned your name."

Judith blushed. "Did you two spend your time discussing me?"

"Not exclusively."

"I should hope not," she remonstrated. "Two grown men with important problems facing them, and they waste their time talking about some girl!"

"A very special girl!" Alan said, bringing her close to him for a kiss. As he let her go and they started for the door, he added, "And don't forget what I've told you about Miles Estey. You're still very much on his mind."

CHAPTER TWELVE

Alan Fraser did himself credit at the meeting of the bridge authority committee. At least Judith thought so. And she was sure quite a few other people did, too. He gave no sign of the strain he was under and no hint of the efforts he was making to attempt to checkmate the North interests. But he did manage to assume an air of confidence and suggest that the various problems might be solved without saying just how.

The Mayor was in attendance, as were bloated Senator Lafferty and several of his associates from the North End Real Estate Owners Association. And in a chair removed from the others, a lone Miles Estey took in all the proceedings. After the meeting, Alan was surrounded by questioning members of the committee, and Judith was left to pack his brief case and get ready for their departure.

It was during this time that Miles came over to her. He offered her a faint smile. "Quite a performance," he said. "I didn't know he was up to it."

She looked at the young labor leader with

a twinkle in her eyes. "He may have other surprises in store for some people."

"I'll be looking forward to them," Miles assured her. "Any reason why you shouldn't drive home in my car?"

She hesitated. "I don't know."

"He's going to be busy here for some time," Miles said. "There isn't any real need for you to stay, is there?"

Judith considered and then said, "Wait until I've given him his papers." She took the brief case and pushed her way through the group around Alan to hand it to him. She said, "I think I'll leave now. We have a long day tomorrow."

Alan interrupted his talk with an elderly woman on the committee to give Judith a surprised glance. Then he looked over and saw Miles waiting and apparently understood. "All right," he said quietly. "No reason you should stay here."

She smiled and went back to join Miles. "I'm ready to go," she said.

On the drive home, Miles told her, "It looks as if I'm going to have to stay here longer than I intended."

"Why?"

"Because it's not clear yet with whom I'm going to be dealing," he explained. "If the Governor takes action on that petition and calls a halt to construction, a new bridge authority will be elected. So there's not much point in coming to an agreement with Alan when he may not be speaking for the authority two weeks from now. I'll have to wait and see what happens."

"There may be no change."

"What makes you feel so sure of that?"

"I can't tell you yet," she said. "But if Alan is successful, you'll know soon enough."

Miles seemed determined to keep his eyes on the road ahead. He said, "Your name came up a few times when Alan and I got together last night."

"So I understand," she said lightly.

Miles showed surprise. "He did mention that to you?"

"Without going into details," Judith said. "Tell me about it. I'm curious."

"Nothing much to tell," the young labor man said awkwardly, "except that I know he's in love with you."

She laughed. "He's been telling me almost the same thing about you."

"Perhaps it's true."

"I thought we'd arrived at a point of understanding," she reminded him.

"I've been considering things since then," he said. "Maybe I don't want to bow out of the race or your life after all."

"I surely hope you won't," she said sincerely.

"I mean that I believe we could still have a future together," he said as they pulled up in front of her place.

She smiled at him. "Right now I'm more concerned about the present than the future."

He gave her a resigned smile. "And more interested in Alan than you are in me."

"I didn't say that," she reminded him. She quickly said good night and got out of the car.

The next day she began her ordeal at the Registry Office. Alan went with her to get her started and then returned to the office, leaving her faced with a seemingly endless search. She had not been working more than an hour when a wizened little man in a shabby blue suit and battered gray hat entered the records room and came up to her.

Removing his hat, he said, "I'm from City Hall. The Mayor sent me. He thought I might be able to help. My name is Foster, John Foster!"

Judith offered her friendliest smile. She pointed to the table strewn with documents. "You know what I'm delving into," she said. "The Harrigan Street properties and those in that area."

"I know well," John Foster said. "Shouldn't present too many problems. I'll just get a stool so I won't have to stand."

Judith was impressed by the wizened man's ability to scan the files quickly and come up with pertinent information. When lunch time came, she asked, "What do you think?"

John Foster gave her a knowing look. "I think we're onto something," he said. And tapping the list he'd started to make, "Nearly every property in that district has changed hands in the past eighteen months. Now it isn't logical that all that real estate activity should go on in one small area without a reason."

"And the reason could be the North End spur of the bridge," Judith said.

"I'd say it has to be," Foster said emphatically. "Some of those houses hadn't changed hands in the previous twenty or thirty years."

"I'll tell Mr. Fraser when I see him at lunch," she promised. "And you will be back?"

"Nothing will stop me," the little man said, putting on his battered hat. "I don't want to miss any of this."

Judith recounted their success to Alan in

the office over a light lunch they'd had sent in. She promised, "By this evening or to-morrow afternoon at the latest, we should have some kind of a picture of what has been going on."

"I think we've got a good hint now," Alan said, holding a half-empty paper cup of milk in his hand as he spoke. "The people we want to get at have been buying up those properties like mad."

She nodded. "So that when the bridge authority has to buy them for a North End spur, they'll be in a position to cash in."

"If only Lafferty is the one behind it and we can prove it, there will never be a North End spur," Alan said grimly.

"It has to be he," Judith exulted. "It all fits!"

"Don't get too excited," Alan warned her. "Remember what happened before."

"We didn't have John Foster to help us then," she told him. "That little man is a wizard."

But even with a wizard to help her, the pace slowed down. It wasn't until mid-afternoon two days later that she and John Foster completed a list of the transferred properties and the parties involved.

The little man sighed. "That's it, Miss Barnes. We've managed all we can here.

There's one company holding most of the better properties, the Northeast Realty Group. And it's headed by a Samuel Kent."

"So Kent is our man," Judith said. "Is the name familiar to you?"

John Foster concentrated, his brow furrowed. "There used to be a lawyer in the North End name of Kent. Must be ancient now. Remember him when I was a boy. But I don't think it could be him. He must be dead."

"I guess it's time for Alan to take over," Judith said, picking up the list.

"Good luck, Miss Barnes," John Foster said.

"And thank you," she told him. "I'll let you know how we make out."

She hurried from the Registry Office and along Canterbury Street to King Street. Since time was all-important now, she was anxious to get the information in Alan's hands as soon as possible. But at the corner she ran into an unexpected delay. She came face to face with Pauline Walsh.

The tall blonde girl was wearing a stylish suit in a loud purplish shade and was as eye-compelling as ever. But her manner toward Judith was not as cordial as previously.

"I've been hoping I'd meet you," she said.

"I'm having some terribly busy days." Judith smiled. "I'm on my way to the office now, and I'm late." She prepared to move on.

But Pauline restrained her with a touch of a gloved hand. "Alan can wait for you just a minute or two longer," she said in a purring voice.

"I am in a hurry," Judith insisted.

"I'm sure you are," Pauline said, too agreeably, "but you can spare a moment for me. Have you heard that Alan and I are no longer engaged?"

"No!" Judith said, genuinely surprised. "No! I hadn't!"

"Strange," Pauline smiled sarcastically, "especially since I had an idea you might be the reason."

"You're wrong about that."

"I'll need more than your word to convince me," Pauline assured her. "But then I don't begrudge you Alan. He's never going to get out of this trouble he's in."

"You think not?"

"I don't suppose you'll mind," the blonde girl said. "But I would feel disgraced." And with that she swept away.

For a stunned moment Judith watched after her. Then she turned and hurried on down the street. So much for Pauline, she thought grimly. She wished that Alan had told her about breaking his engagement so it wouldn't have come as a complete surprise. But she didn't have time to worry about that or discuss it with him just now. There were more pressing matters to be attended to.

She went directly into Alan's office and spread the lists on his desk. "There's the whole larcenous story in black and white," she said. "We are interested in a Northeast Realty Group and one Samuel Kent."

Alan frowned. "Samuel Kent? You don't mean the old lawyer who has his office in a ramshackle building on Elm Street?"

"According to John Foster, that Samuel Kent is dead."

He shrugged. "That's the only one I know. We'll make a few phone calls and see what we can discover."

Judith went out to check the accumulated morning and afternoon mail while he made the calls. After about twenty minutes he came out to stand by her desk with the list in his hands.

"The New England Trust Company is acting as agent for Samuel Kent and the Northeast Realty group," he told her. "They're collecting the rents and taking physical care of the properties and looking after taxes. The balance of monies received after their commission is paid is deposited to an account in the Port Winter National Bank."

"What about Kent?"

"He's not dead," Alan said grimly. "But he's not around here either. He's shut up his office and just vanished into thin air."

"Oh, no!" she exclaimed. "Someone must know where he is!"

Alan shook his head. "According to the Trust Company, he is supposed to get in touch with them. But he hasn't."

"What does it mean?"

"Another dead end, I'm afraid," he said with a sigh.

"Not after all that searching," she said disconsolately. "I can't believe it."

He smiled and patted her shoulder. "You made a good try."

"What next?"

He studied the list. "I'll check with a few of the other North End law firms," he said. "It's possible I may get a lead on this slippery old Samuel Kent from them."

Judith forced herself to settle down to the routine typing of replies to some of the more urgent mail. But she was depressed and unable to concentrate properly. Alan kept on the phone, but she knew that he wasn't having any luck. Soon it was close to five o'clock and closing time. She was about to put away her typewriter when she heard the office door open, and when she looked up she saw it was Brandon Fraser.

The stern, gaunt face regarded her with uncertainty.

Then, in a voice mild for him, he said, "Good afternoon, Miss Barnes. Is my son busy?"

She smiled for him. "He's been making a few phone calls." As she rose to tell Alan his father was there, the young lawyer came out to join them.

"Hello, Dad," he said. "What is it?"

Brandon Fraser cleared his throat. "I just received a call from the manager of the New England Trust Company. He tells me you are looking for a veteran member of the local bar, Samuel Kent."

"That's right," Alan said. "He's important to me because he's been involved in the purchase of a number of properties that will have to be taken over by the bridge authority if the North End spur goes through. And he seems to have disappeared."

"I think I may be able to help you," Brandon Fraser said in the same careful tone. "When he left, he turned a few of his clients over to me. He wrote me about one of them yesterday. And he gave me his address. He's living in a hotel in a small Florida town."

Judith and Alan exchanged delighted glances. And the young lawyer told his father, "I need that address!"

Brandon Fraser carefully drew out a wallet from his inside jacket and then, with equal caution, took a folded slip of paper from the wallet and passed it to Alan. "There it is," he said, returning the wallet to his pocket.

"Delroy Point," Alan said, reading the address.

"I believe it's about thirty miles from Miami," his father said. "You could take a plane directly to Miami and then hire a car and drive to his hotel."

Alan looked up from the slip of paper with a smile. "Thanks for the help, Dad," he said.

Brandon Fraser nodded stiffly and then gave her a meaningful glance before he said in a quiet voice, "That's all right, Alan. I'm afraid it's somewhat overdue." And without waiting for them to make any reply, he turned and went out.

"Well!" Alan exclaimed.

"You'll be needing a witness," Judith told him with a smile. "Do I or do I not get a trip to Florida?"

"You do!" Alan said with enthusiasm. "We can drive to Boston and catch one of the midnight flights. By tomorrow morning we should be in Delroy Point asking Samuel Kent a few interesting questions."

Of course Judith was not able to explain to her mother. A befuddled Millicent helped her pack without really fully understanding what was happening. "What does it all mean? Just tell me why you must rush off this way!"

Judith was glad to be able to give up a hopeless task when Alan came for her in his car. After that events were a blur of wild motion. They'd no sooner driven to Boston than they were aboard a sleek jet bound for Miami. After catching a few hours' sleep on the flight, they were in the modern airport to greet the dawn. They had a hasty breakfast at the airport, and then Alan hired a black convertible for the drive to Delroy Point. As the sun rose, they felt the full blaze of it. It was unpleasantly hot on this June day in Florida. At last they reached the small town. It was a shabby little place off the main tourist route, and the hotel was four stories high with an unhealthy yellow stucco finish. It too had seen better days.

There was air conditioning in the tiny lobby, along with a crabbed desk clerk behind the counter. Alan inquired for Samuel Kent, and the sour man back of the desk put a phone call through to his room. Then he turned to notify Alan the old man would be right down.

Judith set in one of the dilapidated leather chairs, her nerves on edge. Alan stood by her, his eyes on the gate of the ancient elevator, obviously just as shaken as she was. They had worked so long and come so far. In a short time they would know whether the result would be success or failure.

The elevator door creaked open and revealed a dumpy oldster in a white linen suit and a floppy Panama hat. He was leaning heavily on a knobby brown cane, and as he emerged from the elevator with a crab-like walk, his long, blotched face with its flabby jowls worked nervously. His lip quivered as he came to a stop and stared at them. Even from six feet away, Judith could sense the fear in him.

"You want to talk to me?" He had a crafty face, and his rheumy blue eyes were shifty under heavy brows.

"Yes," Alan said, stepping forward. "I'm from Port Winter. You and my father are friends. My name is Alan Fraser."

The old man looked slightly relieved. "You're Brandon Fraser's boy! Yes, I know him. We are old friends."

"That is why I am here," Alan said. "You can help me."

The old man shook his head. "No! I have nothing to do with business these days! I'm retired! My memory is very poor! I'm not able to practice law."

Alan gave Judith a knowing glance before he asked the old man, "Would you rather talk to the police?"

"Police!" the oldster said querulously. "I have nothing to say to the police! I know my rights."

"It might be worth your while to cooperate," Alan went on. "We're not after the money given you by the Northeast Realty group. I don't consider it was enough, anyway. We're only after information."

Samuel Kent stared at him with dark suspicion. "Why should I tell you anything?" And glaring at Judith: "Who's she?"

"My secretary," Alan said. "We mean you no harm. In fact, we think you were given a bad deal. And we want to protect your name in the community."

"I always had a good reputation," the old man in the soiled linen suit sputtered indignantly. "Ask your Paw!"

"He spoke highly of you," Alan went on in his most placating way. "And he said I could depend on you to help."

"He did, did he?" the old man snorted. And then, as if wanting to satisfy his curiosity, he said, "I can't stand here any longer. I'm old and tired. If you want to talk, you can come out to the verandah."

They were seated in three wicker chairs grouped together on the hot verandah. It was now afternoon, and Judith thought she would melt in the heat. Alan was feeling it, too. His shirt was open at the neck, and he fanned himself with a large envelope as he went on trying to convince Samuel Kent to cooperate.

Only the old man seemed to enjoy the deathly heat and thrive on it. He became as alert as a lively old lizard basking in the sun of a favorite desert rock. His rheumy eyes fixed on Alan grimly.

"I don't have to talk," he kept repeating. "They cheated me in the first place after I did all the dirty work. And now you want to double-cross me again."

"Look," Alan said, "as a lawyer, you know you have nothing to fear. You haven't done anything dishonest, nothing you need be afraid of the law for. But the man, or men, you acted for intend to put your work to dishonest use and make an enormous profit — a profit you won't share!"

"I know that." Samuel Kent swung a thin hand at an annoying fly as he replied peevishly.

"You can get even in only one way," Alan raid. "Let me have the name or names, and I'll promise you they won't get away with the swindle they've planned."

Samuel Kent shook his head. "Not interested!"

So it went. He vanished in the evening and refused to come downstairs. They took rooms in a motel a block away that wasn't quite so depressing and suffered through a humid night to pick up the quest on the following day.

To Judith's surprise, the old man came down to join them on the verandah instead of trying to avoid them. And it was only later when he began to ply her eagerly with questions that she realized why. He was lonesome, thirsty for news of his home town where he'd lived so long. She gladly supplied the information, and his mood improved.

Alan was quick to point out another advantage to Samuel Kent. "If this was settled, you could return to Port Winter whenever you liked and no questions asked."

Perhaps this was what won the old man over to their side: the prospect of being able to go back home. But he still took another full day to make up his mind to talk. He began to give them information they needed in the middle of a third blazing hot afternoon.

"All right," he said. "I'll tell you. They've got a full legal transfer to themselves when the time comes. And the Senator has a share in the company, but he's small fry."

Alan frowned. "Lafferty isn't the main one behind it?"

"No," the old man said. "There's someone else bigger than he."

"Who?" Alan asked.

The old man settled back in his chair and started to chuckle. "Well, what do you know about that? He's coming down the street this very minute!"

Judith and Alan looked at each other, certain that they had pushed the old man too far and he had collapsed under the heat and strain. And then she glanced over Alan's shoulder and realized that Samuel Kent had merely voiced the simple truth.

In a taut voice, she told Alan, "Look behind you!"

He did. And there was Councilman Fred Harvey in shirt sleeves with his coat over his arm and wearing a straw hat. He walked slowly up to them, the alert eyes behind the horn-rimmed glasses beaming as usual. The smile on his perspiring face was broad. He addressed himself to the old man first.

"I suppose you told them," he said.

Samuel Kent was still cackling in his high-pitched fashion. He pointed a bony finger at Harvey. "No," he said. "You told them when you walked up here!"

Harvey didn't lose his smile. He turned to Judith. "You were right," he said. "I should have started traveling by plane long ago. It took me too many hours to get here by train. I might have known you'd have it all settled."

Alan said, "I hope you and the Senator are prepared for some important headlines. And you'd better figure out what you're going to do with all the slum property you bought yourself. You're not likely to sell it for a spur to the bridge when this scandal breaks."

Fred Harvey shrugged. "I'm not afraid of headlines. I'm used to being called a crook. And real estate is always a good investment no matter what." He gave Judith a pleasant nod of farewell. "Right now I'm starting to live dangerously, Judith. I'm driving back to Miami and taking a plane from there home!"

They watched him walk back to his car.

Samuel Kent cleared his throat and said, "Well, you've got to hand it to him. He's a cool one!"

Judith laughed. "And I don't think you could say that about anyone else in town when you consider this heat!"

Things worked out about as Alan had predicted. When S.C. North was presented with the evidence that a double-dealing Senator Lafferty, along with Councilman Fred Harvey, had tried to make a huge personal profit on the North End spur of the bridge, the financier quickly lost interest in pushing the spur through. He allowed the scandal to be exposed in his newspapers, with his own share of the scheme to halt the bridge construction discreetly omitted.

Miles Estey came to an agreement with Alan that gave his union workers excellent protection. Perhaps this was one of the contributing factors that led to the giant structure being completed on schedule.

And on the gala occasion of the bridge's opening, Miles Estey returned to Port Winter to take part in the ceremonies. He stood with Judith and Alan on its wide sidewalk, shortly after the ribbon-cutting ceremony. His red hair rippled in the breeze as they watched the initial traffic cross to the

East End of town.

Miles said, "Well, your project is finished, Alan. What next?"

Alan's arm was around Judith. A smile crossed his sensitive face. "There's always a new one. Judith and I are getting married next week."

The tall, red-haired man sighed. "I knew it would happen," he said. "How about calling on the union for a best man?"

Judith laughed. "We intended asking you today."

Miles looked delighted. "I'd say that calls for a kiss for the bride."

Alan tightened his hold on her. "Let me look after that." And as Miles looked on with a chuckle, he did.